THE SAVAGE RIVER

The Pinkerton supervisor told Savage that the job was not dangerous. He must find Miss Beatrice Bottomley, a schoolteacher lost in the wild west. But along the way Savage is jailed, hunted by killers and shot twice. All because Bea was abducted by Foxy Parker's gang of gold robbers. But why is she so important to them? Although Savage faces constant danger, he remains undaunted. His guile, courage and expertise have always helped him win through — but will he succeed now?

SYDNEY J. BOUNDS

THE SAVAGE RIVER

Complete and Unabridged

LINFORD
Leicester

First published in Great Britain in 2003

First Linford Edition
published 2007

The moral right of the author
has been asserted

British Library CIP Data

Bounds, Sydney J.
    The savage river.—Large print ed.—
Linford western library
    1. Western stories
    2. Large type books
    I. Title
    823.9'14 [F] 7896984

    ISBN 978–1–84617–964–8

Published by
F. A. Thorpe (Publishing)
Anstey, Leicestershire

Set by Words & Graphics Ltd.
Anstey, Leicestershire
Printed and bound in Great Britain by
T. J. International Ltd., Padstow, Cornwall

This book is printed on acid-free paper

1

The Prize

'My name's Jay. What's yours?'

This one had a fringe of beard, and a large revolver stuck through his belt. Since she had arrived in the west, a surprising number of young men had courted her; shyly, boldly, silently, garrulously. Back home she had been considered plain; on the shelf at thirty. She had to put her sudden popularity down to the shortage of women here.

Unfortunately, Jay, like all the men crowded aboard the *Lafayette*, had an overripe smell.

Where Miss Beatrice Bottomley came from, the whole family took a bath every Saturday night in front of the fire in the kitchen. Here, she was sure, men went a lot longer than a week without a bath.

'Beatrice,' she admitted, turning from the deck rail. She had been watching the swirling brown water of the Missouri rush past, capped by white foam, as the sternwheeler forced a way upstream.

She didn't add 'Miss' as she had no wish to encourage any of these rough admirers; on the other hand, she knew she was going to need help.

Miss Bottomley was lost. She was forced to admit she had misjudged the breadth of the North American continent, an immensity that appeared to go on forever. She appreciated the freedom, but there was altogether too much of it.

She had, too, misjudged the length of a river that twisted and turned and looped back on itself like a snake. Since crossing the Atlantic she seemed to have lost her sense of direction entirely; the size of this land made her feel insignificant.

'I'll call you Bea,' Jay said, 'and I guess you're from England.'

She nodded. Not only were distances greater than she'd imagined, but also the time spent crossing them seemed to stretch. She was already late taking up her post in Cheyenne, and the trunk with her books and change of clothing had remained on the train when she switched to another line.

'Don't give it a thought, ma'am,' a cheerful black conductor had told her. 'Plenty of labelling on that old trunk. It'll end up at your destination one day.'

But will I? Bea wondered.

She was tired of travelling by railroad, stage-coach and now river-boat, and had been told there was a direct route to Cheyenne when she left this slow boat to Bismarck . . .

The steamer was filled with men in dirt-stained overalls, young, middle-aged and elderly. Their combined smell had driven her forward to the bow where she could lean on the rail and taste fresh, if cold, air.

'You're a miner, I suppose?' she said.

'That's right, ma'am. We're all

miners, loaded down with dust, headed for Bismarck and a good time.'

Miss Bottomley nodded to herself. 'Aye, where there's muck there's brass.'

There seemed to be a lot of muck in the water flowing past, and a dense growth of vegetation on each bank.

'Can't this tub go any faster?' she asked. 'We seem to have slowed to a crawl.'

'No, ma'am, it's the snow-melt we get each spring flooding the river. Only this makes the trip possible — at any other time the river's too shallow for a steamboat. And we're going against the flow.'

She nearly snapped, 'I can see that,' but held her tongue. Most people she'd met in this country had been friendly enough, and some had gone out of their way to help her.

On her own, she'd never have thought of using a riverboat to make a connection and, hopefully, this would be the last change before her destination.

An island showed just ahead, and the steamer took the narrow channel, slowing even more as the pressure of water built up.

'It's deeper this side,' Jay explained.

Branches of trees overhung the channel on each side, big trees growing close together with a tangle of brush between them. It's like a jungle, she thought; anything could be in there.

Minutes later she saw that the trunk of a huge tree had fallen across the water and was blocking the channel. The *Lafayette* slowed still more.

A curse came from the wheelhouse, then a voice bawled, 'Reverse engine!'

The boat stopped and wallowed like a buffalo in the swift-flowing current, swinging from side to side. Gunfire erupted from both banks and, suddenly out of control, the steamer ploughed into a sandbank and stuck fast.

Bea's eyes opened wide; she'd never been shot at before. Jay shoved her violently. 'Get down — lie flat!'

She sprawled on the wooden deck as

bullets whined overhead. Some hit woodwork; some ricocheted off metal.

Raising her head slightly she saw small boats pulling out from the island. Then a piratical-looking bunch of ruffians swarmed aboard, wielding a variety of weapons, clubs and revolvers, knives and rifles.

For a moment there was silence, then Jay muttered, 'Damn, and damn again — it's the Fox!'

Bea was startled. 'What's going on?'

The man who answered looked nothing like a fox. He was tall and broad, with a paunch and a fleshy nose; he lifted a wide-brimmed sombrero and his ugly face split in a wide grin.

'Ma'am, I figure to save these hard-working men the trouble of carrying their gold all the way to Bismarck.'

He spoke politely, but his eyes showed cunning. 'You can get up — the shooting's over.'

He extended a hand, but she ignored it as she scrambled upright. This was not a man she felt she could trust. 'I can manage, thank you.'

He bowed slightly and put his sombrero on. 'I admire a woman with spirit. Oscar . . . where are you, Oscar? Escort our prize ashore.'

She looked around. The captain, in the wheel-house, had ducked out of sight; the rest of the crew had faded into the woodwork. The miners watched in silence.

Only Jay stepped forward, his hand resting on the butt of his revolver.

'Leave the lady alone — she's not your kind.'

The Fox raised an eyebrow. 'You mean there is another kind?'

Before he could answer, a single shot sounded and Jay staggered back, the front of his shirt turning red. His knees buckled and he slid to the deck.

Bea stared, horrified. 'You've killed him!'

The Fox gave a small smile. 'Waal, Nate sure ain't practising for Sunday School.' He turned to regard the young man who'd fired the shot. 'There was no need for that.'

Bea dropped to her knees and felt for a pulse; there was nothing she, or anyone else, could do.

The killer looked no more than eighteen, with blackheads dotting his unshaven face. He shrugged.

'Thought he was going to draw. Anyway, I fancy the gal.' He leered at Bea.

The Fox said, 'I've told you before, Nate — think first, shoot later.' He turned back to Bea. 'This one still thinks with his water-cannon.' He cleared his throat. 'Now, gents, let's get down to business. I'll have your gold and you'll have your lives.'

Furious, Bea said, 'You just wait till I get to Cheyenne — and they're expecting me, so don't think you can stop me — and I'll have the law on you!'

The Fox gave her his attention again. 'That so, ma'am? My name's Parker, mostly called 'Foxy', and well-known hereabouts. You, now, really are a stranger if you think the law operates in this neck of the woods. But I'm curious, just why should anyone be expecting you in Cheyenne?'

'I'm a schoolteacher about to take up a post there.'

'Teacher?' Parker pushed his sombrero back a fraction, then smiled. 'Oscar, get her ashore pronto and on to a horse. Mary-Ann is going to be interested, I figure.'

'Sure thing, Foxy.'

Parker shifted his attention to a couple of miners; a small man being restrained by a big one.

'That's right, big boy. Keep that little rooster under control, then I shan't have to discipline the lot of yuh.'

Oscar stepped close to Bea; an older man, clean-shaven wearing a shiny broadcloth suit and a derby hat. Like all the others in the gang, he had a gun in his hand. 'This way, ma'am.'

'And if I refuse?'

Oscar sighed. 'You've already caused

the death of one man. Ain't that enough?'

'You can't blame me for that!' She looked at him, appalled, then realized he was serious.

Reluctantly she allowed him to take her arm and lead her to the side of the steamer. A small boat was moored there, and he handed her down and jumped in after her. He untied and took up a paddle to guide the boat as the current swept it downstream.

She stepped on to the river-bank while Oscar moored the boat to a tree, and glanced back at the *Lafayette*. Miners were parting with nuggets of gold and bags of dust and didn't look happy about it.

'This way, ma'am.'

Horses and mules waited among the trees, and Oscar asked, 'Can you ride?'

'The only time I've been on a horse was when I was small, and that was a farmhouse pulling a plough.'

'Then I'll give you a mule. All you have to do is cling on.'

Not hurrying, the robbers came ashore and pulled up their boats and hid them among the trees. Nate eyed her.

'You ain't no beauty, but I guess you'll do.'

Foxy Parker frowned. 'Keep your hands to yourself, Nate — Mary-Ann decides what happens to this one. And another thing, why kill a miner? Are you forgetting we need them to dig more gold for us?'

Nate scowled, and the gang loaded their stolen gold on to the mules, mounted their horses and started up between the trees.

The route they followed gradually wound uphill, and Oscar led Bea's mule. She sat awkwardly, side-saddle, as the cavalcade of outlaws rode slowly towards their hide-out; they were relaxed, laughing and joking, their comments coarse. Overgrown louts, she thought, and sniffed.

The forest began to thin out the higher they climbed. She glanced back.

Far below, the river snaked away, a muddy brown; she saw the tops of trees and, among them, grassy valleys, with mountains in the distance.

Her heart sank. She'd never felt so alone. She should feel frightened, she supposed, but this whole affair still seemed unreal. A young man, a stranger, had been shot dead because he tried to protect her . . . these men really were desperados, and she was their prisoner.

It occurred to her that even if, by some miracle, she managed to escape, she would still be hopelessly lost in a wilderness.

★ ★ ★

'Cleaned out!'

Trewin's voice was shrill. He was a small man, and what his voice lacked in volume was made up for by its piercing quality. It held indignation, protest, fury and an urgent need for retribution; he was midget-sized and excitable.

Beside him, Jeff Lamb watched as the last robber disappeared into the forest with their gold. He stayed relaxed as he filled his pipe, a big man calm as a rock.

His voice rumbled. 'You worry too much, Harry. There's always more where that came from.'

'Not for young Jay there isn't.'

The two friends were part of a small group of miners staring down at the body, lying like a lifeless doll on the deck of the *Lafayette*. Some faces were solemn, some sad and others angry.

'He was a damn fool,' one man said, 'but they didn't have to kill him.'

The captain's voice bellowed from the wheel-house: 'If you men have nothing better to do, lend a hand to get my ship moving again. I've a schedule to keep.'

Some of the crew were digging at the sandbank to free the ship; others chopped at the tree blocking the channel; still others fed logs to the furnace to get up steam. The air was blue with some vigorous cursing.

13

'That double-damned Fox! You know what he's like — any resistance and he turns robbery into a massacre. We were lucky.'

'That woman wasn't . . . she'll soon be wishing she were dead. I say it's past time we had some law around here.'

Jeff finally got his pipe packed to his satisfaction, and lit up, but Harry Trewin was like a man with a bee in his pants.

'Forget the law! What we need to do is form a vigilance committee and clean out that nest of vipers. Hang the scum!'

2

Hideaway

Savage was not feeling his best when he unsaddled at the livery at Fremont. It had been a long ride, and he felt like taking it easy till morning. But then he'd have to get up early; better to report in now, and then see if his usual room at the hotel was vacant.

He carried his shotgun and saddlebags along Main to the Southwest and Border Bank, climbed the flight of wooden stairs on the corner and paused on the landing at the top.

The door of the office was open, and a stranger sat behind the supervisor's desk of Pinkerton's National Detective agency. A bulky man in a dark suit, with short fair hair and a neat moustache; a city type, pale skin reddened by the sun. He was smoking a cigar and looked steadily back at him.

'You must be Savage,' he said. 'Come in and sit down.'

He spoke with an accent: English, Savage guessed. 'What happened to Dave Bridger?'

He walked into the office, dumped his gear in a corner and took the chair across the desk from his new boss. Smooth, he decided, and older than he appeared at first; wary, experienced eyes, thinning hair, a moustache stained with tobacco juice.

'Mr Bridger was recalled to New York. My name's Winston, and I'm taking charge here.' The new supervisor glanced at the big Bowie knife sheathed at Savage's waist. 'Is that necessary?'

'Yeah, I like to clean my nails before I eat. D'you know anything about the south-west?'

'No, but I know how to run an office, and I have people like you to run around for me.' Winston smirked. 'I saw your name mentioned in the papers. Got some gold back for the

Government, like a regular little hero.'[1]

It was almost a sneer.

'Mr Allan didn't object to the publicity,' Savage said. 'I received a telegraph from him suggesting I take sick leave.'

Winston shook his head. 'Oh, no. I've a job waiting — and you're the only agent in town right now. You don't look sick to me.'

Savage scowled, wishing he'd gone straight to the hotel.

Winston tapped ash from his cigar into a small dish of water on his desk.

'A schoolma'am got herself lost on the way to Cheyenne and someone wants her found. Her name is Beatrice Bottomley, and she's still missing.'

'How d'yuh know that?'

'Telegraph from Cheyenne.'

'First lost, now missing. A woman travelling alone is always at risk. Was she alone?'

Winston nodded.

---

[1] See *Savage's Feud*.

'So she may be dead, or working on her back in a parlour.'

'So you'll find her and find out, young Savage. This agency is being paid to locate her, and that's why you're paid.' The smirk came back. 'It's not likely there'll be any danger — and a simple job like this should prove no great problem for a trouble-shooter with your experience.'

Winston opened a drawer in his desk, brought out a sheet of paper and handed it to him. 'A copy of the route she proposed to take. Obviously she made a bad connection somewhere. I want you to follow this route and telegraph me from each town.'

Savage studied the hand-drawn map. 'This is outside our area — '

'Even I know that much, but I was handed the job and now I'm handing it to you.'

Winston got to his feet and opened the office safe; he took out a bundle of banknotes and held them out without bothering to count them. 'For expenses.

18

Take the train, and let me know as soon as you find her.'

Savage's hand closed around the money. There was some advantage to a new supervisor, after all: Dave Bridger had been tight with expense money. He shoved the notes in his pocket, collected his gear and paused in the doorway on his way out.

'Will you tell me, Mr Winston — just to satisfy my curiosity — how did you get this job?'

Winston winked and blew a smoke ring. 'Influence, old boy. I was a superintendent with Scotland Yard. Keep in touch.'

Savage clattered down the stairs and headed for the railroad depot, whistling. Now he had money in his pocket his immediate aim was to get out of town. He would stop off some place along the line, where they didn't have a telegraph office, eat a giant-sized meal and sleep for a week; maybe take a woman to bed.

He was in no hurry. Beatrice

Bottomley could stay lost till he was ready to hit the trail again.

* * *

The trees thinned out and gave way to a hillside covered with waving grass, and then to bare earth and stones that ended with a plateau of rock and dust.

Bea, uncomfortable from the long climb spent seated on a worn saddle on the back of a mule, slid to the ground and surveyed the outlaws' hideout.

She knew immediately that what she was looking at had once been a small mining village and was now derelict. The big wheel and the cage suspended above a hole in the ground told her their stories, as did the wooden buildings which were dotted around, most in various states of collapse.

But it was not inhabited by ghosts. As the men rode up with their gold-bearing mules, women and children came from some of the shacks to meet them. The children had long hair, bare feet, and needed a good scrubbing.

A smell of cooking hung in the air, reminding Bea how long it had been since she'd eaten anything. A woman chased a dog running off with a joint of meat. Beyond the village, in a grassy hollow, a few steers grazed.

Perched high up, these robbers were not going to be taken by surprise.

Some of the women regarded her with suspicion, but the kids weren't shy; they edged close, boldly staring and whispering among themselves. Bea gave them a warm smile.

Nate swaggered towards her. 'Beat it, you kids.'

One of the girls put out her tongue. A boy jeered, 'Make us, then!'

Nate drew his revolver. 'I don't want any lip from you lot.'

For a moment, Bea wondered if he would really pull the trigger. Surely not?

Then a commanding voice bawled, 'Put that gun away or I'll flatten you!'

Bea saw a squat, muscular woman

coming towards them. She had grey hair chopped short, and a meat cleaver in her hand.

Nate moved away without a word.

The woman shouted, 'You keep that damned Nate under control, Mister Fox, or you'll end up a man short. D'you hear me? And who's this woman for?'

She wore a pair of men's denim pants, cut off at the knees, and rope-soled canvas shoes.

Foxy Parker smiled. 'For you, Mary-Ann.'

'What does that mean?'

'This lady is a schoolteacher.'

Mary-Ann transferred her attention to Bea. 'Is that right? You teach kids to read and write? What's your name?'

'I teach children, yes, and my name is Beatrice Bottomley.'

Mary-Ann gave her a broad smile. 'You're welcome, Beatrice. These kids need a teacher, and you're it. Mister Fox, get your bunch of worthless, bone-idle bar-room loungers to clean out a hut for her to use as a schoolhouse.'

She swung around. 'Beatrice, do you have books and stuff?'

'Not with me — my trunk was lost somewhere along the way.'

'A trunk? Properly labelled?'

'Yes. It should eventually arrive at Cheyenne. As I should.'

Mary-Ann ignored the final remark. She looked with a critical eye over Parker's gang and made her choice.

'You, Oscar, go collect the lady's trunk from Cheyenne.'

Oscar started to protest, then glanced towards Parker, who nodded.

'Better do what she says, Oscar. She's got the bit between her teeth over this schooling — we'll never have any peace till she gets what she wants.'

Swearing under his breath, Oscar walked away. 'I'm eating first,' he shouted back.

Mary-Ann made a face. 'I'm forgetting — you're likely hungry, Beatrice.'

'I could eat a horse!'

Mary-Ann nodded approvingly. 'There's nothing wrong with a nice piece of horsemeat.'

The town kids closed in a ring around Bea, apparently fascinated. One asked, 'Are you really a teacher, Miss?'

Another laughed. 'Why would a teacher come here?'

Mary-Ann glowered. 'She's come here to teach you lot so you'll be polite and address her as Miss Beatrice. And you'll do what she tells you.'

A boy with freckles piped up: 'Miss Beatrice, ma'am, can you read to us, please?'

Bea smiled. 'I can, and I will, when I have my books.'

'I've got a book, Miss.' He produced, from behind his back, a dime novel with a lurid cover.

'What's your name?' she asked.

'Luke, Miss.'

Miss Bottomley beamed. 'I can see you're going to be my favourite pupil, Luke — a boy who *wants* to read!'

* * *

When Savage finished his breakfast — pork and beans, with two large cups of coffee — he decided it was time to move on. His woman of the night had begun to cloy ... 'Call me Trixie, 'cause I know a lot of tricks.'

His body was healing fast and his brain insisted that something didn't feel right about the current job. Who was it wanted this schoolteacher found? Why? Who was paying the agency?

He settled the hotel bill, collected his saddlebags and shotgun, and walked to the depot to wait for the next train.

Suspicious by nature, he considered his new supervisor: an English detective who gave out a minimum of information. He felt sure Winston knew more than he was telling. Maybe he'd reveal more when Savage telegraphed him.

He bought a ticket. The train arrived with a whistle and a clanging and clouds of steam, and he boarded and found a seat on his own. He put his feet up, pulled the Stetson low to cover his eyes, and left his hand resting on the haft of his knife. Each time someone passed by, his eyes flicked open. Savage was not a man who could relax entirely.

His early life as a boy, an orphan surviving on New York's waterfront, had taught him to sleep like a cat. Always hungry, he stole to eat; a loner, he relied only on himself.

He had slept in any dry corner sheltered from the weather. This night it was an empty warehouse, and his bed a nest of newspapers and cardboard. He gripped a chef's knife, sharp as any razor, in his hand.

A shuffling of feet alerted him. It was not yet fully dark, and moonlight shone through a glassless window. Silently he came upright, moving to one side, watching shadows.

A cajoling voice, a deep voice, echoed eerily through the emptiness.

'I saw yuh, kid. I saw you grab that wallet. Real slick. Share with me and I'll see you right. You're quick and I'm strong — share and share alike, kid. You can trust me.'

Savage smiled briefly. He trusted nobody, least of all this shambling figure with long arms everyone called 'The Ape'. Strong as a gorilla, if he got his hands on anyone it ended with broken bones. He could snap an arm or leg as casually and as easily as another man might break a stick of candy.

Savage backed slowly away from the giant shadow looming before him. The Ape was between him and the door; the windows were too high to reach, and the door at the far end was locked and chained.

He had no intention of sharing his loot. He'd taken the risk and he'd enjoy the benefit. In the darkness he transferred the few dollars it contained to his pocket and held out the empty wallet. If he could tempt the Ape away from the door . . .

He tossed the wallet on the floor as a decoy and prepared to sprint when the giant reached for it.

The Ape laughed. 'I ain't that soft in the head, kid. Gimme the money, or I'll grind your bones for glue.'

Cloud covered the moon for brief seconds. Savage threw his knife and swerved to get past those grasping hands.

He barely made it. Glancing back, he glimpsed the Ape with the haft of a knife projecting from his throat, and ran for his life.

'Bloody little savage,' the Ape gurgled . . .

Savage stirred, shedding a dream of the past before he was blackmailed into working for Allan Pinkerton. He had one bit of luck before the train reached its next stop, when he questioned a black conductor.

'Remember a lady travelling alone to Cheyenne?'

'Yessir, I surely do. An English lady. She got herself real upset 'cause she lost her trunk. That went on without her, but was clearly labelled, so it'll arrive one day.'

'And where might she be now?'

The conductor rolled his eyes towards heaven. 'You ask the Almighty that one, sir. Only He knows.'

English? That was something Winston hadn't mentioned. What the hell was he playing at? Was the Bottomley woman a criminal? Was there a reward out for her?

The trail was cold when the Northern Pacific dropped him off at Sioux City. The town was busy, the railroad delivering people, the hotels filled with trappers and their furs and miners hoping to strike it rich. He passed Indians wanting money for liquor, and soldiers waiting for trouble.

No one he spoke to remembered an English woman teacher aiming for Cheyenne, but this was a drifting population, always on the move.

It didn't help that Savage was a stranger to the area and so never considered the river. He soon got fed up with experts recommending a sure-fire way to reach Cheyenne, each method different.

In the end he decided to quit hunting the woman. He'd go directly to her destination and, if she still hadn't arrived, work backwards from there.

3

Crazy Riders

Kelly could walk through the doorway of his office without stooping if he didn't wear a hat. Outside, he slammed his hat on his head, tugged down the brim, and adjusted the hang of his Colt.

A man who interested him had just passed the open door of his office, riding a horse and leading a mule; a stranger to Cheyenne.

Kelly didn't hurry. His long legs could move fast when necessary, but he wasn't expecting trouble. He watched the rider stop outside the new schoolhouse, across the street, and dismount.

Kelly strolled easily along the boardwalk, his gaze missing little. Although he refused to wear a star on his shirt — 'a target for gun-happy cowboys', he called that — a narrow oblong of metal

31

carrying the word MARSHAL was discreetly pinned to one lapel of his coat.

A thin man, by turning sideways, he figured to avoid a fatal wound.

The stranger was talking to old Ernst, a member of the school board. Ernst had lost an arm and was glad to get any kind of paid work. Just now he didn't look happy, and his voice carried.

'You want to collect her trunk? Where is she? Why isn't she coming?'

Ernst saw the marshal watching and called out, 'This *hombre* claims Miss Bottomley sent him to collect her trunk.'

Kelly nodded; he knew the expected schoolma'am was overdue. He crossed the road leisurely, studying the stranger.

He saw a middle-aged man wearing a shiny suit and derby, clean-shaven; he might have been a visiting drummer. The revolver shoved in his belt under his coat was not unusual for men in the west.

'He's been telling me our teacher got a job someplace else and won't be arriving,' Ernst said with a scowl. 'I can't see any point in holding her things if she ain't coming.'

Kelly, not one to waste words, nodded again. 'Anything of value?'

'No, just schoolbooks and women's clothes.'

The stranger seemed a mite uneasy under the marshal's scrutiny. 'She met an old friend,' he explained. 'The friend fixed it so she didn't have to travel further.'

Kelly inclined his head. Maybe, maybe not, but his jurisdiction ended with the town limits, and no crime had been committed here. 'All right.'

He recrossed the road and walked back to his office, removed his hat and sat just inside the door, watching the street.

Presently he saw the stranger pass by on his way out of town, but now the mule had a trunk strapped to its back.

Kelly sighed, went to his desk and

spent some time leafing through a thick wad of Wanted notices. His dream was that one day he'd catch a notorious criminal and make a name for himself.

★ ★ ★

'We know what men are, don't we?' Mary-Ann said, and sniffed.

Bea nodded in agreement. 'Oh yes, I've read a bit of history and — '

They were sitting in the shade, each with a glass of lemonade, overseeing some of Parker's crew as they cleared out and repaired a hut to use for a schoolhouse; one large room for a teacher and pupils of every age. The men worked without enthusiasm.

' — they always seem to be off fighting somewhere, killing and looting, and leaving us at home to do the real work.'

'Exactly. But they have their uses.'

Nate approached them, grinning. 'How about a kiss, Bea? All this work is for you.'

She looked through him. 'Why don't you take a cold bath?'

Mary-Ann added, 'Yes, why don't you? After you've finished this job, of course.'

Nate muttered under his breath and kicked a stone, but returned to work.

Mary-Ann said, 'Mister Fox will have trouble with that one, if he isn't careful.'

Bea was curious. 'But not you?'

Mary-Ann laughed. 'Not me. I can handle men.' She flexed her muscles. 'I was married to a wrestler at one time, and I learned a few holds and throws. I run this town, and the only time Mister Fox is the boss is when the men are away on a job.'

As Bea silently contemplated the kind of job Parker did when he was away, a tall thin girl — perhaps sixteen, Bea guessed, too old for school but not yet a woman — hurried around the corner of the building. She was out of breath, her face pale and her body tense. She had a sharpened stick in her hand.

'You leave Nate alone!' she screeched. 'He's mine, so leave him be or I'll poke your eyes out!' She flourished her stick in Bea's face.

Mary-Ann spoke sharply. 'Quit that, Ethel — he's not worth it.'

'I'll decide that,' Ethel retorted.

Bea said, 'You're welcome to him. I'm not interested.'

'Liar! He's interested in you and — '

Bea moved quickly, grasped one end of the stick and wrenched it from Ethel's hand. She took hold of a skinny shoulder and spun the girl around. Ethel gasped as Bea laid the stick across her behind; it wasn't a regulation teacher's cane, but it would serve.

'Behave!'

Ethel was startled and ran off, sobbing.

Mary-Ann snorted. 'That useless Nate chases every woman, and treats Ethel like dirt. She's a fool to put up with him.'

'Perhaps,' Bea said. 'I've seen young

girls with a crush before. She'll grow out of it.' And she thought, if someone doesn't kill him first.

* * *

As Oscar rode out at one end of town, Savage arrived by rail at the other. He stepped down from the coach, carrying his shotgun and saddle-bags and looked about him.

No New Yorker ever admitted to being impressed by any hick town, and Cheyenne had only recently put the sod hut stage behind it. There were still boardwalks and frame houses, but he saw one brick building going up as he left the depot. He stopped at the first hotel he came to, booked a room for the night and relaxed over a meal.

Afterwards he stepped out to find the law office. Why not? He was a detective, and the marshal should know what went on in his town. He strolled between women shoppers and business-men, past idlers outside a saloon and

37

turned in at a door with the sign: TOWN MARSHAL.

He introduced himself and his mission to a long, thin man at a desk piled with Wanted notices.

The marshal stared at him. 'A Pinkerton?' He seemed overwhelmed. 'Hunting a schoolteacher?'

Savage waited for him to recover; a nameplate on the desk read: K. KELLY.

'One who's gone missing, Mr Kelly. She was due here — I suppose she hasn't turned up?'

The marshal shook his head slowly; he seemed to be considering something, so Savage waited.

'Overdue. Fellah collected her trunk.'

'Did he say where she is now?'

'Nope.'

'Did you see which way he went?'

'Headed out across the plain.'

'When was this?'

'Earlier today.'

'Then I guess I'll head that way too. Did he give a reason for her change of mind?'

'Yep. Can't say I believed him.' Kelly studied Savage carefully, then shrugged.

'Anything distinctive about him? How was he travelling?'

'Looked like a drummer. Had the trunk on a mule.'

It was like extracting teeth, Savage thought; why would a drummer collect a teacher's trunk? 'Where can I hire a horse?'

Kelly hesitated. 'Hire? Maybe buy. There's no law in the Territory — you're on your own.'

He watched his visitor leave, then went through the Wanted notices again with renewed interest.

★ ★ ★

Oscar reined in his horse a mile beyond Cheyenne and twisted in the saddle to look back towards town. He was relieved to see no one following him. That marshal had been suspicious but, luckily, had enough savvy to stay inside his territory. Some he'd known in the

39

past ignored boundaries, and would have been camped on his trail.

He urged his mount forward again, passing a stand of timber and heading out across the empty prairie. Mary-Ann had been right to pick him for this job; some of Parker's gang looked exactly what they were, and might have had trouble collecting the teacher's trunk. He still looked enough like a drummer to get past the law when required.

Three years ago, he'd been a drummer, trying to sell tools in towns across the west; a hard life for little reward. Working for Foxy paid better, and he was appreciated as a front man.

He wondered what would happen to the teacher. She wasn't bad-looking by western standards, so someone would be sparking her soon. He couldn't see her teaching kids for long, despite Mary-Ann.

As he rode on, he realized he wasn't getting any younger and that it might be pleasant to settle down with some home comforts; maybe he'd throw *his* hat in the ring for her.

⋆ ⋆ ⋆

The plain beyond Cheyenne stretched to the horizon, the short brown grass of winter beginning to turn green and grow again. The trail Savage followed appeared to be well used in places, and hardly used at all in others.

The combination of horse and mule tracks were distinctive and not hard to find; and once he met a rider coming towards him, so he paused to exchange greetings and ask the man if he'd seen anything.

'Sure thing, partner. *Hombre* with a trunk on a mule — some way ahead of yuh.'

It appeared the man he was following was in no hurry, so Savage didn't push his mount; best to let him lead all the way to wherever the Bottomley woman was.

It was also the first time he'd bought

41

a horse, and he didn't know enough to judge. The seller had assured him the pony had stamina, but he didn't want to find out the hard way that he'd been sold a dud and end up walking.

He continued at an easy pace over the seemingly endless prairie until a bunch of riders cut across in front of him. Unsure of them he slowed down; their zigzag wandering puzzled him.

When the riders became aware of him, they wheeled about and headed towards him. Minutes later he realized they were Indians, half-naked and painted, with feathers in their hair. He'd heard a lot about Indians, but the only ones he'd met were Little Owl and his band.

These men showed they were hostile by charging; they screamed their war cry and fired their rifles.

Savage's blood quickened, and he pushed his horse to a gallop; the Indians came whooping after him. He'd heard tales of lone white men caught by the Sioux and didn't want to meet a painful end. He swung up his shotgun and pushed off the safety, but held his fire. Let them get close first.

His horse seemed as keen as he was to leave the Indians behind, but one brave was catching up on him, waving a scalping knife. Savage aimed low and squeezed the trigger. The Indian pony bucked wildly and threw its rider.

Immediately, two others dropped back out of range. Don't fancy a shotgun at close quarters, Savage thought grimly, but he was still puzzled by their actions.

Some of them chased him, firing blindly; it was apparently only by chance that a bullet came near him. Other braves raced through an arc to get ahead and cut him off, and then lost interest. Had they been chewing loco-weed?

Savage's horse kept going flat out, and Savage clung on. One Indian tried to use his bow and got it tangled up with the blanket on his pony's back. He was laughing like a maniac. This is crazy, Savage thought, leaning forward across his mount's neck.

Hoofs thudded as another brave came thundering alongside. It seemed he was trying to jump from his pony on to the back of Savage's, and he fell sprawling to the ground between them as Savage swerved aside.

That was when he realized they were drunk, and stopped worrying.

He'd heard of traders selling whiskey to Indians even though it was against the law, but this was his first experience of the result. Eventually they tired of harassing him and dropped behind.

Savage let his horse take a breather, and then rode on. During the chase the land had changed; the plain led towards a range of hills thick with trees.

He began searching for the tracks of a horse and mule again when he saw a group of buildings on the horizon, close to the base of the hills. Maybe here he would get news of Beatrice Bottomley.

4

Crosstrails Chandler

The saloon was big and crowded, smoky and noisy, yet Harry Trewin's shrill voice cut through the atmosphere like a saw through timber.

'We must form a vigilance committee to get rid of Parker and his pack of murderers, and we must do it now!'

Some of the miners drinking had glum faces, some showed anger, others gave him a cheer. They hadn't forgotten Jay, or previous raids that had left them poorer.

'Duck' — when he waddled it was obvious where his nickname came from — thumped the bar counter. 'I'm for it — we must stop that gang, or they'll take everything we've worked for, including our lives. I'll gladly swing for the Fox myself!'

There was a roar of approval and shouts of agreement, in principle. Jeff Lamb puffed on his pipe and listened. Harry was excitable and had to let off steam; like many of the riverboats, if he didn't have a safety valve, he'd explode. Jeff stayed relaxed, ready to haul his partner out of trouble.

A doubtful voice challenged Trewin. 'Big talk, little fellah, but how are yuh going about it? Follow them into the hills?'

'We'll decide how later,' Harry said quickly. 'Are we together on this? Can we agree to form a committee?'

He heard a chorus of 'Ayes', and said, 'Now all those in favour of taking direct action?'

A forest of hands sprang up; more cheering.

A man with his own bottle said, 'I'm with you.' The speaker was tall, and dressed as a riverman. 'I owned two boats and now I've got one. Parker destroyed the other one and murdered my crew. Count me in.'

Harry began, 'I've got an idea how — '

Jeff laid a big hand on his friend's shoulder. 'Not now, Harry, not here. Keep it to yourself.' He put his pipe back in his mouth.

Harry looked startled until Duck said, 'That's right — we don't know who's listening.'

The riverman laid coins on the counter and told the barman, 'Set up drinks for everyone.' As drinks were poured and hands reached for glasses, he spoke quietly.

'Follow me. We'll adjourn to some-where more private, just a few of us, to discuss ways and means.'

He settled a peaked cap on his head and strode outside. Harry, Jeff and Duck followed him into the night to plot how to outfox the Fox.

★ ★ ★

As he approached the collection of shacks, Savage realized they marked a spot where two trails crossed the prairie; another track, barely visible, led up into the hills.

Some of the log cabins were old and patched with roughly sawn planks; a few were newer. There were posts stuck in the ground and wire strung between them to form a corral.

The main building, a long hut, was large and weathered and a prominent signboard proclaimed: CHANDLER'S STORE.

On the New York waterfront, he remembered a chandler sold ship's stores. A smaller sign read:

Buy, Sell, Exchange
Rooms, Food, Whiskey, Ammunition
Marriages performed: Burials arranged

Seeing pigs rooting among the shacks, and chickens scratching, he dismounted and turned his horse into the corral. He carried his shotgun with him when he walked inside the big store; there was an area where a few men sat at tables, drinking and smoking, watching him in silence. One of the men was an Indian.

Savage paced the length of the hut, between racks of guns, barrels and wooden crates; tinned goods were stacked on shelves, and hams hung overhead. Bare spaces were filled by advertisements for tobacco or playing-cards.

The man behind the counter screwed up his eyes the way sailors do when looking into the sun. He had wrinkled skin the colour of a walnut.

'A meal,' Savage said, 'and a quart of coffee.'

'Two bucks,' Chandler said, holding out a hand. 'It's a long ride to anywhere cheaper.'

Savage paid him, noting the tattooing on his forearm as the storekeeper reached out to take the money.

'Anything else you want?'

'Just some information,' Savage said casually. 'Am I far behind a drummer with a trunk on a mule?'

Chandler's expression became blank. 'Who's asking? Would you want me to inform on you to the next rider to call here?'

Savage bared his teeth. 'I was chased here by Indians, liquored up — maybe you sold them the whiskey?'

'If I did,' Chandler said calmly, 'I probably saved your life. They were Sioux.'

'You damn well know it's against the law to sell whiskey to Indians!'

'Law? What law?' Chandler spread his hands, appealing to his other customers. 'You *hombres* see any law around here?'

This got a laugh, and Chandler continued, 'In case you can't read, fellah, I'm a trader. I sell anything to anybody — travellers, Indians, outlaws — even lawmen if one should happen by, though that's not likely.'

Savage let his gaze roam around the long room; he saw coffee and flour and dried fruit, men's long johns and wide-brimmed hats.

There was nothing obviously out of place; nothing to suggest an English woman teacher might have visited here recently.

Chandler's customers watched to see which way he'd jump. One, dressed as a cowboy, eased his revolver in its holster; a couple of others silently disappeared, not wanting to be involved.

Savage deliberated. Obviously Chandler must have helpers around; the amount and variety of stock indicated he wasn't running a one-man show.

He kept his voice mild. 'Have you seen a school-teacher? An English woman?'

Chandler's eyes opened wide. 'A teacher? Here?' His voice expressed disbelief, and he brought a length of knotted and tarred rope from beneath the counter and slapped the wooden top with it.

'Kid,' he stated, 'if you're funning me, don't. When I was ship's captain, I broke in a dozen like you.'

There was a time when Savage would

have lost his temper over the 'kid'. He smiled coldly. 'Not many ships around — '

'That's where you're wrong. We ain't far from the Missouri, and riverboats still work it in season.'

The Missouri. Savage realized he'd missed something, maybe something important. 'From where to where?'

'I sell information,' Chandler reminded him, and Savage laid a couple more dollars on the counter, and waited.

The storekeeper stared at him. 'Exactly who are you, mister?'

'Just somebody looking for a teacher who's disappeared.'

'Waal, I ain't got her, and I've never set eyes on her — the river runs from Kansas City up to Bismarck, and some boats go further when there's enough water.'

A voice cackled, 'If Foxy doesn't stop 'em!'

Savage turned to an old man sitting alone at a corner table and holding an empty glass. 'Foxy?'

The oldster mumbled, 'Talking's thirsty work.'

Savage nodded to Chandler. 'Give him another.' He waited while another beer was poured and carried to the old man.

'Foxy Parker — got himself a quick-shooting bunch who hold up the boats to take gold off'n miners. And women, if any are stupid enough to travel.' He leered.

It's possible, Savage thought. She didn't arrive at Cheyenne, so she went somewhere. A smell of cooking made him salivate. 'Has Parker raided a boat lately?'

'Heard tell some fool got himself shot on the last boat,' another voice joined in.

'Where will I find Parker?'

This question stopped the conversation. Even breathing sounded loud in the silence, and Chandler looked startled. Apparently no one had gone looking for the Fox before; it seemed folk avoided him as if he had the plague.

Suddenly, Chandler laughed and jerked a thumb in the direction of the hills. 'Up there,' he said, 'if what I hear is right . . . here comes your meal.'

An Indian woman came from a kitchen out back, carrying a plate of eggs with slices of ham.

'Eat hearty,' Chandler said, 'and enjoy every mouthful. This may be your last meal! The odds are too high against for any of us to bet on your coming back.'

★   ★   ★

Mary-Ann kicked off her shoes and waggled her toes. She sat in the shade of the school hut, listening to the voice of Beatrice Bottomley as she instructed her first class.

This gave Mary-Ann a feeling of satisfaction; a school was something she'd nagged Mr Fox about for months and she really felt she'd achieved something. Now she'd got the school started, she intended to keep it going.

And that, possibly, was going to be just as hard. She'd noticed the way some of the men watched her teacher. They didn't hang around when she was about, but she could see what was coming. Beatrice was so far unattached.

In some ways, Mr Fox was a fool. Sure, it was safer to keep men away from saloons where there was a danger of liquor loosening tongues — men were inclined to boast, she'd noticed — but pressures built up. And not only for men.

For the present, Beatrice was avoiding the men, but that wouldn't last. Mary-Ann still remembered her own youth, and taking her first man in her uncle's barn. But Beatrice was older than she'd been and, at a guess, without experience. One day she'd feel she was missing out on something, and then Mary-Ann wanted to be firmly in control.

In the meantime, she needed to come up with some distraction, to direct the men's attention away from her teacher.

* ★ ★

Savage had confidence in his horse and let it pick its own way up the barely discernible hill track. Trees grew thickly, blocking the view until he was high above the plain. Then he found the horse and mule tracks again. He glimpsed the Missouri river in the distance, a brown snake winding its way between the hills. The trees thinned to give way to a grassy slope.

He rode on, alert, shotgun resting across his saddlehorn, when two look-outs showed themselves, covering him with rifles.

The bigger of the two challenged him: 'Where d'yuh think you're going, stranger?'

Savage swung his shotgun around and sat easy. 'I'm looking for a man named Parker. Heard he resides up this way.'

The other look-out chuckled. He had a weasel face and puffed on a hand-rolled cigarette. 'Waal, you got that right. We'll escort yuh, seeing we ain't had much fun lately.'

He motioned Savage to continue uphill, and the first man said, 'You'll be welcome. Foxy reckons to let simple folk like you provide entertainment. It sure gets a mite dull up here, just admiring the scenery.'

They closed in, one on each side. Both had a brutal stamp to their features and were well armed. Savage ignored them.

The track became bare earth and rock, and then flattened to a plateau. He saw the ruins of a mining village; derelict huts and an open shaft with a cage suspended over it.

'It ain't ghosts you've got to be scared of,' Weasel-face said, as other members of the gang gathered around.

'Hi, Foxy, you've got a visitor!'

Savage watched a large, paunchy man wearing a sombrero stride towards him, and said, 'I'm looking for Beatrice Bottomley. Is she here?'

5

Whose Body?

Foxy Parker stood facing Savage. He ignored the question. 'Who the hell are you?'

'Name's Savage.'

'Waal, Mr Savage, since you're here, put the safety on your gun, and slide it into its scabbard, then get off your horse.' He paused for one heartbeat. 'Which idiot allowed him to ride in here with a loaded shotgun in his hands?'

The two look-outs eased to the back of the crowd as other men pressed close about Savage, eager hands helping sheathe the shotgun and pull him from the saddle. Obviously they were not used to visitors calling.

Revolver muzzles jabbed his flesh, but Savage remained calm. 'Why all the excitement? I only asked if the

Bottomley woman was here.'

Parker rubbed the side of his fleshy nose, watching him with hooded eyes. A sly one, Savage thought, waiting.

'Someone bring her here,' Parker said at last.

'I'll get her.' A pimply youth hurried towards the huts.

Savage looked around casually and saw women and children; it was clear that Parker had a small town here.

'How d'yuh get here?' the gang leader asked.

'Just followed your man who collected her trunk in Cheyenne.'

Parker swore. 'You, Oscar, what's the matter with yuh? Letting someone follow you — '

Savage saw for the first time the man whose tracks had led him here; a middle-aged man, clean-shaven and wearing a derby.

'Am I surrounded by idiots?' Parker's face was suddenly ugly. 'I ought to — '

The pimply youth returned, urging a woman forward, and Savage saw the teacher he'd been searching for. No beauty, but mature; she looked freshly scrubbed and wore a long creased dress. Recently bathed and changed, he thought, since she got her trunk.

She appeared calm, though her face was flushed, and he guessed she was apprehensive.

Parker said, 'Beatrice, you have a follower. Claims his name is Savage. D'you know him? Have you ever seen him before?'

She looked at Savage with interest, a searching look, and then shook her head. 'No, I can't recall the name, and I haven't seen him before.'

Parker laughed nastily. 'What d'yuh say to that, Mr Savage?'

Her accent was English, Savage thought, similar to Winston's; but he wanted formal identification.

'Are you Miss Beatrice Bottomley, a school-teacher, from England?'

She nodded, and Savage said, 'I've been hired to find you.'

She was startled. 'Hired? Who paid

you? Who would do that for me?'

Parker added, 'Yeah, who sent you?'

Savage shrugged. 'I've no idea,' he admitted.

Parker's eyes glowed. 'Then we'll have to refresh your memory, won't we?'

From the *Kansas City Star:*

MYSTERY CORPSE

Sheriff McKittrick is appealing for help in identifying a murdered man. The unknown victim was found in the early hours, just beyond the railroad depot and close to the track.

He had been shot once with a .41 calibre revolver at close range. Apparently no one heard the shot, and there is no lead so far as to the murderer.

The dead man was middle-aged with white skin, and probably a recent arrival in the west. No identification is possible from clothing, because he had been stripped to his underwear.

The sheriff said: 'He might have been a passenger on the train from Chicago, travelling south-west, which stopped to take on water during the hours of darkness. Do you have a husband or male relative who is missing?

If you have information that might lead to identifying this unknown man, please get in touch with the sheriff's office as soon as possible.

'Last chance. Who's paying you?'

Savage didn't dare mention the Pinkerton agency; these men wouldn't hesitate to kill anyone even remotely resembling the law.

Foxy Parker said, 'All right, we'll — ' He stopped and frowned, as the men crowding around Savage began to chant, 'Fight, fight!'

Savage didn't like the sound; it

reminded him of hounds baying for blood. A hand snatched the knife sheathed at his waist.

Bea looked fearful; she didn't know what was coming, but she remembered Jay being shot down without a chance.

The pimply youth said eagerly, 'Let me!'

Parker regarded him with contempt. He looked Savage over and said, 'He'd eat you alive, Nate.'

'You take him, Foxy.'

The rest of the gang continued to chant, 'Fight, fight!'

Parker sighed. 'Yeah, all right, but — ' He studied Savage closely. ' — I figure this is one for Mary-Ann.'

'Who is?' a voice demanded. 'What's going on, Mister Fox?'

Savage turned his head to see a woman marching towards them. She had a squat, powerful body and greying hair chopped short. Maybe forty, he guessed. Her shirtsleeves were rolled up, and her denim pants cut short; her forearms and calves bulged with muscle.

As the men began to chant again, excitedly this time, she saw Savage and pushed through the crowd to look him over.

'He's young,' she said doubtfully, and the men gave way before her. She stepped up close and felt his biceps, smacked his stomach muscles. Her expression changed to one of interest.

'Maybe.' She addressed Savage directly. 'Are you any kind of a fighter?'

'I'll fight any man present.'

'Man,' Mary-Ann said, and smiled. 'Who is he, Mister Fox? Where'd you get him?'

'Claims he followed Oscar here — claims someone paid him to find Beatrice.'

She stared at Savage. 'Who paid you?'

'I don't know,' he repeated.

She raised an eyebrow, calculating, deliberating. 'All right. I'll fight him.'

A cheer went up and Savage realized this was their main entertainment. He was half-pushed, half-carried to a cleared patch of bare earth, shaped roughly to a square. The crowd lined the crude ring and he was pushed inside. Faces were flushed with excitement. Somebody called out, 'I'll take two-to-one on Mary-Ann,' but there were no takers.

Savage watched her scuff the ground with her canvas shoes; the rope soles would give her a firm grip. She looked tough and solid, and he'd never fought a woman before.

'My game's wrestling,' she told him.

Savage nodded curtly; he could see no obvious way out, so he'd have to go through with it. He told himself he needn't pull his punches; she'd fought men before.

Beatrice Bottomley watched with an anxious expression.

He took a long breath and stepped into the centre of the ring, and Mary-Ann came directly at him. He still found it difficult to take her seriously, and put up his hands in front of him in a defensive position. She closed fast and gripped his wrists; his feet left the ground and he soared through the air over her shoulder.

He hit the ground and rolled away. Even so, the fall jarred the air from his lungs.

'Come on, get up,' a voice from the crowd urged. 'One throw shouldn't hurt a tough kid like you!'

Savage climbed to his feet and circled her. Obviously she was no beginner at the wrestling game; he moved warily, but not warily enough.

Again she seized his wrists and levered, and again he hit the ground with bone-jarring force and spat out dust. The watching men began to jeer, and he lost his temper. He sprang upright and rushed her.

'Bad move,' Mary-Ann said as she caught one arm and swung him around and around until he was dizzy; suddenly she released her hold.

Savage crashed into a bunch of cheering men forming the ring, and was roughly pushed back.

'Make a fight of it,' a man told him. 'You're not even trying!'

He crouched, looking for an opening. It was no use fighting her way.

'Come on, fight!' yelled the crowd, bloodlust rising. 'Break some bones, Mary-Ann!'

He lashed out with his boot, trying to knock her off-balance. His ankle was caught and twisted painfully, and he went down again.

Nate laughed. 'Jesus, I could do better than that!'

Savage scrambled up, hands clenched, and rushed in; one good punch and —

She wasn't there, but her out-thrust leg tripped him and he went down, rolling. His bruises hurt. The ground was rock under a thin layer of dirt — and Mary-Ann was hardly working up a sweat.

This time he stayed down, waiting, and when she approached, he grabbed at her calf; the muscle might have been carved from stone.

She made no attempt to break free,

but fell on top of him, making use of her weight, grabbed his hair and banged his head on the ground till he lay there, half-stunned.

She leaned close, mouthing words quietly as she pretended to chew his ear. 'Give in before I break something!' She winked, 'Next time I throw you, don't get up. Act dazed. Understand?'

It wouldn't take much acting, he thought.

She rose in one easy movement and stood back, waiting. Despite jeers and an invitation to 'Have a go', Savage took his time getting to his feet. As he sucked air into his lungs and flexed his muscles, he realized he had to make this look good.

He decided on a rush, aiming a blow to her head but intending, at the last moment, to hammer her stomach.

Again he found his arm trapped. As his feet left the earth, she whirled him around and hurled him to the ground. This time he stayed down, cursing his sore muscles and the bruising he'd taken. He made a half-hearted attempt to rise, and flopped back.

His mouth full of dust, he croaked, 'You win', and lay still. The crowd of men laughed and jeered.

Mary-Ann smiled, picked him up and slung him over her shoulder. Beatrice Bottomley followed as she headed for the hut they shared.

'Not right now, Bea. You stay with the kids — that's what you're paid for.'

Bea paused, startled. 'Paid?'

'Why not? We've plenty of gold. You'll get your share, don't worry.'

Mary-Ann carried Savage through the doorway and dropped him on her bed. The door banged after her and he heard laughter outside. She regarded him critically.

'Guess you're still in working order, even if you do look like something a dog dragged in. Strip and wash, kid.'

There was a bucket of water in one corner, and Savage shed his clothes and washed down. Mary-Ann stripped off and lay on the bed, and he found he was interested despite his aches and bruises.

She was no longer young, but had breasts the size of melons, wide hips, and a nest of dark hair between her thighs. He didn't bother to dry off, just climbed on top of her.

'That's the idea,' she encouraged. 'Get your own back — I ain't fighting.'

Her legs clamped around him. 'Go it, youngster!'

She was eager, and he kept pumping till she wrestled him on to his back and mounted him. 'My turn now.'

Savage was beginning to pant. She was no lightweight, and obviously hadn't been properly serviced for some time. She seemed inexhaustible until, eventually, he collapsed.

'That's better,' she said cheerfully. 'Now, tell me about your interest in our Beatrice. Who's paying you?'

'I've told you, I don't know who. Or why.'

'Don't get stubborn with me.' She punched him lightly.

Savage countered, 'I'm wondering how Bottomley got here when she was supposed to be arriving at Cheyenne.'

His gaze was caught by a lump of yellowish ore on a shelf. If that was solid gold . . . he realized there must be a fortune here for the taking.

'That's an easy one. She was travelling on a riverboat that Mister Fox raided. His men tend to grab any woman travelling that route. Your turn again.'

'I've simply no idea who's paying to find her. I wasn't told.'

Mary-Ann sighed, slid off the bed and began to dress. 'You're too stubborn for your own good.' She raised her voice. 'He's yours, Mister Fox.'

Savage got up hurriedly and into his clothes. If Parker was going to try any rough stuff, he wanted some protection.

6

Caged

The door was jerked open from the outside and he saw a crowd of grinning faces. Mary-Ann gave Savage a shove and he stumbled through the opening to be grabbed by eager hands. He got in two quick punches before someone clubbed him from behind.

Foxy Parker said, 'Put him in the cage. That'll soften him up.'

Hands went through Savage's pockets and took what was left of his expense money. He was dragged towards the mine shaft. Someone opened the door of the cage and he was thrust inside; the gate closed on him and a chain was wound around the bars and padlocked on the outside.

Parker tipped back his sombrero and asked, 'Feel like talking?'

Savage, more or less conscious, ignored him. One man tugged on a rope that went over a pulley, and the cage lifted off the ground. Another worked a ratchet that swung the cage over the dark hole; it hung suspended there.

Savage thought it could have been worse, until he noticed that the rope holding the cage was beginning to fray. He wondered how deep the shaft was.

Parker's men gathered around, laughing. He recognized Oscar and Nate and the two look-outs.

He sat down, cross-legged, in the middle of the cage and tried to relax, to keep calm and wait them out.

They didn't like being ignored, and pushed sharpened sticks between the bars to prod him. He moved back, but the cage began to sway and he remembered the frayed rope, so sat down again.

He soon became aware of the sun beating down; the corrugated iron roof did not shade all the cage. The vertical iron rods forming his prison were hot and blistered his hand when he touched one. The base he sat on was solid timber, inches thick.

One of the men was drinking whiskey from a bottle and offered him a drink. Savage was not a whiskey man, but liquid was liquid. When he reached for it, the man turned the bottle upside down and emptied it on the ground. That got a laugh.

The sun seemed hotter, and he became aware he was starting a thirst; he could survive without food, but not long without liquid. The cage began to feel like a pan in which he was frying.

Eventually the robbers got tired of mocking him and, one by one, they drifted away. Left alone, Savage felt a fierce anger starting to build in him. Caged like an animal — this had never happened to him before — someone was going to pay for it.

Shadows gathered, and he supposed they were eating an evening meal, and drinking. His throat dried up at the thought — and then the English schoolteacher came hurrying towards him, a large dish held in both hands.

She had difficulty getting it between the bars, and tilted the dish, spilling some of the precious liquid. Savage got his mouth under it and drank greedily. He passed the empty dish back. 'Thanks.'

'I can't stay,' she murmured, and hurried away.

He licked his lips and felt better; she had given him a chance to survive.

Presently a few kids gathered around the cage, trying to reach him with sharpened sticks, but their arms weren't long enough. He sat watching them.

A lone steer detached itself from the small herd in the hollow and made for the kids at a trot, horns lowered. Immediately they lost interest in Savage and turned on the animal, dodging its horns as they jabbed their sticks at it, tormenting the beast. It was a game to them.

They darted away at each toss of the

horns, scattering as the steer pawed the ground and made a furious charge. They ran into shacks to hide, and the animal gave up and retreated.

Darkness came. The village grew quiet. Savage curled up in the bottom of the cage and slept till the cold woke him.

* * *

'Eat up,' Mary-Ann said. 'This high, the air will give you an appetite. And you're going to need something solid inside you to handle our kids.'

Bea had not spent a good night, worrying over what might happen to Mr Savage; these men were murderers, she remembered. She had a bed in Mary-Ann's hut, who slept as if she didn't have a care in the world.

Bea had already washed, dressed and made up her bed before Mary-Ann cooked breakfast. She usually had a healthy appetite, but the amount of steak Mary-Ann had fried looked

76

intimidating. Quite right, of course; she was going to need all her strength for what lay ahead.

Her life had taken a strange turn. It seemed that anything she asked for could be provided, including food in vast quantities; and she had no need to worry about money. It could have been an idyllic life — though she was puzzled by Mr Savage's claim of being paid to find her. Why should he lie? There was no one she knew of to care whether she lived or died.

She began to eat and discovered that, after all, she did have an appetite.

Mary-Ann beamed. She was in good humour after her love-making with Savage. 'That's right, Beatrice, eat hearty while you can, and any little problem, see me.'

From outside came excited voices, children's voices, shouting and laughing. 'What on earth's that?' Bea asked.

Mary-Ann winked. 'Just high spirits. Let them wear themselves out and they'll be easier to handle.'

Then Bea heard men's voices encouraging them. Metal rang as something hit it. They were doing something to Mr Savage, she thought, and pushed back her chair and went outside.

She was horrified. She saw kids throwing stones at him. Savage was lying flat on the bottom of the cage to avoid them; some struck the metal bars, making them ring, but others got through.

'Stop that at once!' she ordered, striding towards them.

The younger children obeyed. One of the older boys said, 'He ain't hurt — it's just a bit of fun.'

Bea ignored him. 'It's time to begin class, so you will all go into the school hut. Now.'

The same boy grabbed one of the smaller girls and twisted her arm. 'Not you, sis. You don't have to take any notice of her.'

'Mary-Ann said to.'

Bea cuffed him around the head. 'If you don't stop bullying your sister, I'll send *you* to Mary-Ann.'

For the moment she had control and, slowly, they moved towards the school hut. She followed, refusing to notice the men's laughter.

The children chose their seats, and Bea closed the door and took her place in front of the class. They were still restless. She picked up a school-book, and paused; she couldn't stop thinking about poor Mr Savage in the cage, and put the book down again. She had first to capture their attention.

'Luke,' she said, 'you had an adventure story you wanted me to read from — '

'Here, Miss Beatrice!'

The freckle-faced boy rushed up to her and held out a battered dime novel with a lurid illustration on the cover and titled, *A Hero of the Prairie*. She browsed through the pages, looking for an exciting bit.

She chose a late chapter, headed 'Dangerous Dan to the Rescue', and began to read aloud:

Dangerous Dan was on the trail of the red devils! He pushed his magnificent stallion to a gallop as he followed their tracks from the burnt-out covered wagon.

Behind him, among the dead and mutilated bodies of his travelling companions, a dying man had begged him with tears in his eyes to save his daughter, Nancy, who had been taken captive.

Dan rode like the wind across the prairie until he spied the tents of their camp. His eagle eyes spotted Nancy easily by her golden tresses. She was tied to a stake, and half-naked braves danced around her, waving scalping knives.

Dan galloped fearlessly in among her captors, knife in hand, his great stallion knocking them flying. With one slash of his knife he freed Nancy, hauled her across his saddle and rode for his life.

The stallion was strong but carrying double-weight, and the

red devils, howling their rage and threatening revenge, chased him across the plain, intent on a double scalping!

Dan laughed as he rode. He had kept his promise to rescue Nancy, and nothing else mattered.

Beatrice Bottomley paused in her reading and looked up. She saw a fascinated audience, silent and intent.

'Not mocking a prisoner, or throwing stones, or bullying someone smaller,' she said. 'That's not how a hero behaves. And you do all want to be heroes, don't you?'

* * *

It was getting dark again. Savage squatted like a small motionless Buddha, trying to subdue his raging thirst by will-power.

He picked up a small pebble that one of the kids had thrown and sucked on it, staring at his tormentor, the pimply-faced Nate.

'You ain't goin' to get out, fellah. Foxy'll keep you there till yuh talk, then lower you down and leave yuh. It don't take long for anyone to scream their way crazy down there in the dark.'

Nate laughed; he'd given up trying to jab him with a sharp stick. Savage had grabbed the end and pulled him off balance, so Nate had almost gone down the open shaft.

The moon disappeared among a bank of cloud and Nate was boasting again. 'If it was up to me, I'd shoot yuh right now.'

He lifted a rifle threateningly, so Savage assumed he was duty sentry. Unnecessary, he thought, but Foxy was a wary one; probably he was assigned night-duty as a punishment.

He detected a rift in the gang. 'But it's not,' he said quietly. 'Parker gives the orders, not you.'

Nate scowled. 'Not for ever. We youngsters have other ideas. Maybe it won't be long before I take over.'

Savage suppressed a smile. Take over from Foxy, the sly one? Not this year . . .

A soft voice called from the shadows, 'Nate? It's me, Ethel.'

A thin girl in a skimpy dress moved into view as the moon came out again, and Nate lost interest in baiting Savage. He saw she was alone and pushed her back into darkness.

Savage heard the rustle of clothing, a giggle. 'Don't tear . . . wait!' There was a squeal of rusty hinges. 'In here.'

Savage's anger had been building steadily. He hated Parker for caging him; he hated Nate for baiting him. Before long he would be tempted to do something reckless, anything to get at them.

Would the teacher bring him another dish of water? Something moved in the darkness; it was a lone steer, sniffing the ground, perhaps the same one the kids had been tormenting. It merged with the shadows.

Time dragged. The moon shone

silver for a few minutes, then clouds hid it again. In the dark, Savage didn't feel a bit sleepy.

He heard footfalls, and Beatrice Bottomley glided into view, empty-handed. Without a word she worked the ratchet and swung the cage away from the shaft; she loosened the rope, and it hit the ground with a thud.

Savage held his breath. No one came to investigate, and he offered silent thanks to Ethel for keeping Nate's mind off guard duty.

He watched Bea remove a pin from her hair and work on the padlock; she bent it this way and that while Savage sweated and forgot his thirst. Her face wrinkled with concentration, and he realized she wouldn't hear anybody approach; he kept a sharp watch, exercising his muscles so he'd be ready.

Then he heard a metallic *click* as the ward turned. The moon shone on her face and he saw relief there. She carefully removed the chain.

'These men are desperados, Mr

Savage. They murdered a young man aboard the riverboat — I couldn't stand by and let them murder you, too.'

She jerked open the cage and Savage stepped free.

'Thanks,' he croaked.

'Did someone really pay you to find me?'

Sounds of movement whispered through the night and Savage didn't answer. His gaze fixed on Ethel, adjusting her dress, and behind her, Nate, his pimply face contorted in the moonlight as he brought up his rifle to shoot.

7

A Challenge

Savage pushed Bea violently. 'Get away from me!'

She went sprawling as Nate loosed a shot that went wild; it's not so easy aiming by the light of the moon as cloud passes across its face, Savage thought. He stepped back, so the grounded cage gave him cover.

The young outlaw triggered again and shouted, 'The prisoner's out!'

Savage was edging back towards deep shadow when he glimpsed a new threat. The rogue steer the kids had been tormenting came trotting towards him, horns lowered, snorting.

He darted to one side as Nate fired and, desperate for any chance, grabbed at the nearest horn as the animal charged past. He was dragged along the ground until he managed to throw one leg over the steer's back and heave himself up.

He snatched at the other horn, levering the steer around to aim its bulk at Nate as he took aim again.

Nate sprinted for safety as the maddened beast chased him, shouting an alarm as he ran.

Savage clung on grimly, pulling at each horn in turn to hunt down his tormentor. He glimpsed Bea, standing well back in the shadows.

Oil lamps flared in windows and men moved into the open with guns. Time to go, he thought, and aimed the steer for the path leading down to the plain and kicked its flanks to keep it moving.

The animal gave him a rough ride, trying hard to shake him off. It rushed headlong downwards, skidding on loose stones and ricocheting off trees. It snorted and bucked, and lashed its tail, trying to get at the man on its back.

Savage listened to the sounds of pursuit; men were following close behind, and the noise the steer made in its furious descent made him an easy target. Shots winged past his head.

He waited till his unusual mount reached dense undergrowth, and then, as the steer dug its hoofs in, allowed himself to be thrown clear. He rolled into cover as the animal rushed on.

He lay still in the dark as horsemen swept by, chasing the steer, then crawled deeper into the undergrowth and away from the track. He moved slowly because the canopy blotted out the moon's light and he could barely see where he was going.

He paused now and again, listening. He could hear men shouting in the distance; and another sound, the trickle of water over pebbles.

He moved faster, not worrying about the noise he made; his throat was parched as a desert. After a very few minutes he lay face down, lapping at ice-cold water. He moistened his lips and tongue before drinking a little; only then did he take great gulps.

When he'd finished drinking, he retraced his steps towards the main trail, selected a suitable tree and climbed it. Resting on a stout branch that had enough leaves to hide him, he waited.

The sound of returning horses drifted to him; so they'd discovered he was no longer aboard the steer. Angry voices complained, 'The bastard must be here somewhere. Split up and find him.'

Riders moved between the trees, searching, forcing a way through the undergrowth.

Above them, silent and motionless, Savage waited in the gloom. He needed to make his move soon, but he wanted one man on his own.

Minutes crawled past, then came the shadow-shape of a horse and rider moving slowly, hunting him. Savage waited till they were directly below, and then dropped from his branch.

He knocked the hunter from his saddle and rolled on top of him; the man tried to struggle, to shout, but the air had been forced from his lungs. Savage knocked the hat from his head and scrabbled at the earth with his free hand.

He found a lump of jagged rock, raised it high and smashed the man's skull. He stood, smiling grimly. One of them paid back.

He searched the man's pockets and removed a roll of notes, settled the Stetson on his head, and looked around. The horse, reins dragging the ground, grazed quietly.

He caught up the man's body by the ankles and pulled it into some shrubbery to hide it until he'd got clear, then swung into the saddle and eased a rifle from its scabbard. He headed downhill, passing a shadowy rider coming up.

'Thought I heard something lower down,' he muttered as he went by.

When he reached the plain, starlight seemed bright as day, and he urged the horse to a gallop.

Beatrice Bottomley tried to remain calm. She'd lost sleep, but was glad Mr Savage had got away.

After breakfast, she stepped out of the hut she shared with Mary-Ann to walk to the school-house, only to find Foxy Parker and some of his men waiting for her. Her heart skipped a beat.

Parker stared searchingly into her face. 'Thanks to your interference, the prisoner got clear away. Do you still claim you don't know him? Or who paid him to find you?'

'I released Mr Savage, yes. I did so because I feared for his life. I never met him before, and I can't imagine anyone paying him to find me.'

Mary-Ann appeared quietly beside her. 'She comes from a different country, Mister Fox. Naturally, she takes a different view of us.'

Parker tapped the side of his fleshy nose. 'I'm not stupid, Mary-Ann, just puzzled.'

'Perhaps you should question your night sentry,' she suggested.

Nate spoke quickly, pointing at Bea. 'It was her — I saw her plain enough.'

'But you didn't stop her releasing the prisoner,' Mary-Ann said. 'Why not?'

'It was afterwards.' Nate's face turned sullen. 'I was patrolling the other end of town. One sentry can't be everywhere.'

Bea kept quiet. Although she'd recognized Ethel, she didn't want to get the girl into trouble with Foxy Parker. She glanced towards the school hut where her pupils were gathering, staring towards her and listening intently.

Nate took a deep breath and said, 'If I had been in charge, this wouldn't have happened. I'd have killed Savage straight away.'

Parker regarded him thoughtfully. 'Are you questioning my decision?'

Nate glanced around. A number of young outlaws clustered behind him, ready to back his play. 'I'd do things differently. We've never had a prisoner escape before.'

'True,' Parker agreed quietly. He gave the impression he might be carefully considering this challenge to his authority.

Another youngster added, 'And he killed Todd.'

Parker nodded. 'That's true, too. Perhaps I should stand down and let the young ones show what they can do. All right, Nate . . . you can lead the next raid, you and your young friends, right? I'll take a back seat.'

He walked slowly away as Nate's hotheaded friends crowded around him, noisily proclaiming what they'd do when the time came.

Bea was surprised; and even more surprised when she saw Mary-Ann studying Parker's receding back. The matriarch was shaking her head and smiling.

★ ★ ★

The riverman led the way from the saloon to the waterfront and along a footpath where boats were moored. The sky held a sprinkling of stars, and few lights showed aboard the boats.

The evening air was quiet. Away from the saloons, rivermen were not a rowdy lot.

'My name's Russell,' the riverman said, 'and this one's mine, the *New Victoria*.'

Harry Trewin saw twin smokestacks rising against the sky and heard water lapping gently at a stern paddlewheel; the boat was moored fore and aft, with no illumination. He followed Russell up the gangplank.

'That you, Russ?' A brawny figure loomed from the shadows.

'Aye, brought a few friends back to share a drink.' Russell entered the main cabin and lit a kerosene lamp. 'Sit down, everyone, while I pour drinks. I've a decent bourbon — an advantage of working the river is you get to pick your suppliers.'

Duck sighed happily. 'Bourbon for me.'

Jeff Lamb filled and lit his pipe. The cabin showed signs of a previous splendour, but since its early days had been used to transport more than gamblers and wealthy sightseers. The gold paint had faded, the fretwork was damaged, and the velvet plush stained and torn.

When they were settled, Russell said, 'You can speak freely here — my men are keen to avenge their friends. You've got your committee, Harry. Now let's hear your plan.'

Trewin took a small swallow to oil his throat. Russ was right; he'd got hold of the real stuff. 'I'll keep this simple. We set a trap — '

'Using what for bait?'

'A rumour. We start a rumour your boat's carrying gold next time — is that all right with you?'

'Aye,' Russ said, 'if it means we lay our hands on the Fox.'

'The rumour reveals the day you'll be

starting out.' Trewin's eyes gleamed; he was getting excited again.

Jeff took the pipe from his mouth. 'How can we be sure word will get to Parker?'

'A careless word is all it takes,' Duck said. 'A careless word in a saloon will get back to him — and this time we'll be ready for him!'

* * *

Savage kept riding at a steady pace till the sun came up. He'd felt tempted to stop for a meal at Chandler's, but, suspicious by nature, he decided against it. It seemed unlikely the crosstrails storekeeper could operate where he was without collaborating with Foxy Parker; and Savage wanted the boss outlaw to remain unsure of his present where-abouts.

Once out of sight of the store, he allowed his horse to set the pace and save it, and he headed for Cheyenne.

This was the nearest place he was

sure had a telegraph office, and so from there, he could let Winston know he'd found the missing school-ma'am.

After that it was up to the supervisor. Bottomley had done him a good turn, but that didn't mean he had to rush to her rescue. She had kids to teach, so what did it matter who or where they were? However, the raiders had a hoard of gold that *did* interest him.

He moistened his horse's lips from the water bottle; fortunately there was a full one strapped to the saddle close to a loaded Winchester.

He rode on until he saw a small wagon camped beside a stream, and a solitary figure cooking over a fire. The man glanced at him without fear.

''Light and eat, partner — 'less you're in a hurry, of course.'

'No hurry,' Savage said, dismounting. 'That smells good to me.'

He let his horse graze with the pair from the wagon as his host placed more rashers in the pan over the fire and poured black coffee into a mug and handed it to him.

The wagon driver was no youngster; he had grey whiskers, a thin face and wore a shiny top hat.

Savage drained the mug and held it out for a refill. He noticed a weathered sign on the side of the wagon:

DOC CURE-ALL
Medicines, for every complaint
Stomach powders
Teeth pulled
Herbal remedies

Doc appeared friendly; he had an easy manner and a casual air, and pressed him to more bacon and beans.

Gradually, Savage relaxed. He'd got the measure of this man now. He'd seen similar types back East; they were rarely violent but somehow, the money in your pocket ended up in their pockets. He felt almost at home.

'I'm aiming to take in Cheyenne,' Doc said.

'Me, too.'

'In that case, sir, we might travel together, for company. I believe this to be Indian territory.'

'I got chased by a bunch,' Savage admitted, 'but they were the worse for drink.'

'Luckily,' Doc said, reaching behind him and holding up a bottle, 'we're safe!'

He harnessed his horses and Savage saddled up and rode alongside the wagon. From time to time he checked his back trail but there was no sign of pursuit.

'That your horse, kid?' Doc asked.

Savage smiled, pleased he no longer reacted violently. 'It is now. The fellah who rode it before was aiming to put me down.'

'Real careless of him,' Doc commented.

Conversation languished as the sun rose higher. The hours passed without incident and Savage was surprised when they rode into town because almost the first person he saw, taking his ease in a wicker chair on a hotel veranda, was his new supervisor.

Winston looked out of place in smart city clothes, his face still raw from the sun. He was smoking a cigar and stood up as he recognized the rider.

Savage wondered who was running the office back in Fremont. He reined to a halt as Doc Cure-all drove on as though they were total strangers.

'I trust you have news for me, Savage?'

'I found the teacher, if that's what you mean.'

Winston looked pleased. 'That's good. Come inside and tell me about it over a meal.'

Savage hitched his mount and joined him; as they entered the hotel he saw Marshal Kelly approaching along the boardwalk.

Savage followed Winston into the dining-room and ordered, 'Coffee now, steak with all the trimmings to follow.' He was still aware of a parched throat.

But the Pinkerton supervisor couldn't

wait for him to finish his meal. He leaned forward with an eager expression. 'Where is she?'

Savage paused half-way through his steak. 'Up in the hills, with a bunch of gold-robbers.'

Winston listened intently as he filled in the details between mouthfuls, mentioning the trail leading up from Chandler's store.

As Savage finished eating and called for more coffee, he asked, 'So who's paying us to find her?'

Winston ignored the question. 'Is she still there?'

Savage nodded, wondering what was coming. He saw Marshal Kelly come through the door as Winston stood up.

'That's what I need to know . . . he's all yours, Marshal.'

8

Fiasco

Savage set down his coffee cup with care. Marshal Kelly had a big revolver in his hand and his hand was steady, the muzzle pointing directly at him. He almost reached for the rifle propped against the wall beside him, but thought better of it.

As Winston walked out through the door, other diners paused in their meals to watch.

'Stand.' The tall marshal got behind Savage's chair and picked up the rifle with his free hand.

'Is this some kind of joke?'

Kelly prodded his back with the gun muzzle. 'Stand, I said.'

Reluctantly, Savage got up. Kelly stepped back, still covering him, and Winston had disappeared. He was on his own. 'What's going on?'

'Walk.'

Savage's temper was rising. 'You know I work for the Pinkerton agency — '

Another jab in the back. 'Keep walking. That's not what that Pinkerton supervisor says.'

Savage's feet moved slowly as he wondered what hand Winston was playing now.

Outside the hotel, the marshal said, 'To the jail.'

Savage tramped the boardwalk, coming to the boil as townspeople hastily removed themselves from his path. But he needed facts. 'What story did this supervisor tell you?'

'Said you were wanted for murder, back East — and that you are dangerous.'

'The last bit's true, not the other.'

'Natural you'd say that.'

They passed Doc Cure-all standing on the seat of his wagon and flourishing a bottle. A small crowd had gathered around him, mostly women. Doc ignored Savage as he walked past under the marshal's gun, and called in a voice loud and clear:

'Ladies and gentlemen, this small bottle comes to you with my personal recommendation. A tonic for the nervous system. I am not asking five dollars, or even two. I am so confident of it — '

Savage reached the jailhouse and Kelly pushed him into a cell at the back. The door was already open and a key in the lock. The marshal swung the iron door shut, turned the key and pocketed it.

Savage faced him, gripping the bars. 'Are you taking his word, just like that?'

'Until I've made enquiries. You settle down — there's no hurry.'

Isn't there? Savage thought, and didn't feel like settling — except with Winston.

His head was in a whirl, wondering why the Englishman had done this to him. Whatever he was after must concern Beatrice Bottomley — yet she denied him — and, obviously, he didn't want any interference.

So Winston was due for a surprise just as soon as he got out of jail; his feeling towards his supervisor was turning vicious.

He crossed to the window and tried the iron bars. There was no give in them, but he was in time to see Winston driving a buggy out of town.

* * *

Nate scratched at a blackhead till blood trickled down his face. He was near the bottom of one of the trails leading from the old ghost town Parker had taken over, keeping a watch on the river. According to the news that had reached Foxy, the riverboat was almost due and was carrying enough gold to make a raid worthwhile.

The Fox had kept his word. He, Nate, was in charge, leading a bunch of young outlaws keen to prove themselves, primed and eager to act. He heard a hum of excited chatter behind him and said curtly, 'Keep the noise down.'

Spike sniggered. 'You want to bet they can hear us? Those wood-burners are real noisy.'

Nate felt irritated. He was their leader, and they ought to take him seriously.

If anything went wrong, Foxy was going to lay the blame on him; he had no doubt at all about that. He brushed aside a branch carrying a mass of broad leaves to peer out.

The river was shallow at this point; a deep channel ran close to the bank, while submerged rocks and sand further out meant the pilot had to be extra careful. So far, the river was empty and the only sound was that of fast-running water.

He turned to face his gang of young men, most not yet twenty; some sprouted dark stubble, and all were eager and excited about pulling their first job on their own.

Nate swatted at a fly that kept pestering him. 'Listen. Forget what Foxy said — I'm in charge here. We're going in hard, ready to shoot at any sign of resistance — and shoot to kill. Show them straight off that we mean business. No hesitation, no fooling around. And we shoot to kill if they're slow about handing the stuff over.'

'And any women they've got on board?' someone at the back said.

'Them too.'

Nate doubted there would be any women since the teacher had been taken. News like that got abroad, and the few women around would be even more reluctant to travel by boat.

He heard a rhythmic pounding and hissed, 'Be ready!'

The noise grew as he watched the bend in the river. He saw first a cloud of dark smoke, then tall smokestacks, and finally the bow cleaving the water as the pilot swung towards the deep channel and the bank. He saw firemen feeding logs to the furnace . . . but there were few men on deck, and he frowned. The boat was not crowded with miners as it should have been.

It steamed nearer, and he strained his eyes to read the name: *New Victoria*. It was the expected gold shipment. The paddlewheel at the stern turned slower as the pilot started to negotiate a tricky bit. The deck was almost level with him, and Nate realized that if he was going to board her it had to be —

'Now!' he shouted, and ran forward, revolver in hand.

His bunch of young outlaws came to their feet and surged after him. Someone fired a shot across the bow.

'Board her!'

As Nate reached the spit of land closest to the boat, the air was suddenly alive as if a nest of hornets had been disturbed. Or so it seemed. Then he realized they were bullets being fired from the *New Victoria*.

There were more men on deck than he'd thought, but they were lying flat behind barrels and crates and iron plates, and they were equipped with rifles and shotguns.

Pellets shredded the leaves around him, and something stung his cheek. His men wavered. They'd expected to surprise the crew — but somehow the boat was full of armed men triggering lead as fast as they could. It was the raiders who got the surprise.

The fusillade sounded deafening at close range; a continuous barrage that rolled like thunder. One youngster cried out as lead spun him around.

It's all going wrong, Nate thought. Desperate, he fired back, trying to rally his men. It was a trap, he realized, and felt sick with dismay.

'Goddamn it!'

He was suddenly alone and exposed, and turned and ran after his men, already in full retreat. He raved and swore as he ran, and bullets flew after him.

There was nothing to do except follow the young outlaws up the hill path. The raid had failed. Some didn't even bother to grab a horse or mule.

Nate passed one of his men limping after the others. 'Slug in the leg,' Spike moaned. 'Help me!'

Nate passed him and ran on. In this situation, it was every man for himself. Spike cursed him.

Frustrated and disappointed, Nate began to worry what Foxy would say . . .

'They're running,' Harry Trewin shouted. 'After them!'

The New Victoria was still moving, but slowly and close to the bank. The small miner leapt ashore, rifle in hand, stumbled, then set off up the hill track.

Captain Russell called out, 'I can't leave my ship — give 'em one for me.'

Duck, a coil of rope over one arm, waddled after Harry, encouraging other miners to follow. 'We'll sure put the Fox out of business this time!'

They set off in pursuit, firing their guns as they went. Jeff Lamb frowned. Harry always got overexcited. He put his pipe in his pocket and followed after them; someone had to keep his partner out of trouble, and he owed him one.

He never forgot the time a bunch of miners went down with burning fever when there was not a doctor within fifty miles. He was one of those who survived when others were dying all around him; and he survived because Harry stayed to look after him, brought him clean water, and nursed him when he was helpless. Even in his moment of triumph, Harry was likely to rush in without thinking.

The hill track became steeper and the leading vigilantes grabbed a wounded outlaw, disarmed him and knocked him to the ground. Duck uncoiled his rope and fashioned a noose in one end.

'That's the idea,' Harry shouted. 'Hang him high!'

When Jeff arrived, he protested, 'This one's only a boy.'

'Maybe,' Duck said, throwing the other end of the rope over a branch, 'but he's carrying a man's gun.'

Spike looked scared, and pleaded, 'I was just doing what I was told — '

'Stop whining, son, and take your medicine like a man,' Harry said, as Duck adjusted the noose about Spike's neck. 'Time for your last prayer.'

Duck laughed as the youngster wet his pants. 'Haul him up, boys!'

Jeff tried one last time. 'Think what you're doing!' he urged. 'You're going to get the Fox mad at you.'

Another miner chimed in, confidently, 'We can deal with Foxy.'

Several men grabbed the rope and hauled on it, and the young outlaw was strangled as his feet left the ground. Duck tied the end of the rope to a tree trunk.

'That's the first one — come on, let's nail the others.'

With Harry and Duck leading, the vigilantes swarmed up the hill. Jeff Lamb sighed and followed.

★   ★   ★

Savage paced his jail cell, restless, his fingers curling as he imagined getting them around Winston's neck. He was still brooding when he heard someone walk into the jailhouse.

'G'day, Marshal.'

Savage stopped his pacing to listen. He knew that voice: Doc Cure-all had come visiting.

'I always like to pay my respects to the local law when I hit town.' Doc removed and polished his top hat. 'Just so we understand each other. I'm not the kind of cheap crook you're entitled to run out of town, no sir. I'm the genuine article. My pills and potions work.'

He paused, lowering his voice. 'What I'm offering you, Marshal, entirely free of charge, is a bottle of whatever you need. Do you have a headache? A bad back? A gimpy leg? Upset stomach? Or maybe it's your wife? In that case I can offer — '

'Not interested,' Kelly said, in a flat tone of voice.

113

'Waal, maybe there's a local tax on visiting salesmen? Say, five bucks?'

Kelly showed a prompt interest. 'Ten.'

Doc appeared worried. 'Ten? That's — ' His gaze wandered to the prisoner in the cage at the rear of the jailhouse, and not by a flicker of an eyelid did he reveal that he'd seen Savage before. 'Say, who've you got there?'

'A murderer.'

'That so?'

Doc pursed his lips and gave Savage his full attention. 'Waal, now, what's that old saying? 'The condemned man ate a hearty breakfast'. I'll tell you what, son, as you're going to the gallows I'll do you a favour. Just hand over whatever money you've got in your pocket, and I'll bring you a slap-up meal from the best hotel in town and a bottle of wine to go with it. I can't say fairer than that.'

'That's robbery,' Savage grumbled, feeling in his pocket for the roll of notes he'd taken from Parker's man. 'But why not? I've no other use for it.'

He held out the banknotes and, as Doc reached between the bars, felt something small and hard drop into the palm of his hand. He refrained from looking at whatever it was, just hid it away as Kelly snapped, 'Get away from there!'

Doc moved back with the money in his hand.

'It had better be good,' Savage said.

'Oh, it will be,' Doc assured him, and peeled off two five-dollar bills and handed them to the marshal with a wink.

As he walked out through the doorway, he added, 'It'll be the best meal I've had for a while, at your expense.' He settled his top hat on his head. 'Remember that other saying? 'There's one born every minute!'

He went on his way, chuckling.

Marshal Kelly inspected his prisoner, who held out both hands to show they were empty then: then Kelly returned to his file of Wanted notices. He had another face to look for now.

9

Gift for a Jailbird

Foxy Parker waited patiently, sombrero tipped forward to keep the sun from his eyes, and rifle close to hand. All his men carried rifles as they waited, not necessarily patiently, at the top of the hill where the trail from the river left the trees.

Their guns covered the open area between the trees and the plateau; and there were some who wondered why the Fox had let Nate lead the latest raid.

Parker took another sip from his water bottle. One or two of the men were smoking. They were used to waiting beside the river for a boat to show, but this was something new. Foxy's memory went back to another time of waiting, in a canyon, in pouring rain . . .

★ ★ ★

He was the youngest of the gang, and it was his job to hold their remounts ready to change over. Gene and the rest were in town waiting for the bank to open.

When they got back, hopefully carrying sacks filled with notes and coins, they were likely to have a posse at their heels. So, Foxy thought, that made him the most important member of the gang. And planning to take over.

He smiled as rain dripped from his hat. Even the weather favoured him. It would provide a veil to cover his actions.

He heard a drumming of hoofbeats and knew the gang was returning. Peering through the rain, he recognized Gene in the lead. The bank-robbers came in a bunch, vaulting from the saddles of tired horses, grabbing the reins of their fresh mounts.

Parker heard more horses coming; a posse, and not far behind.

Gene snapped, 'Quick, man — they're almost breathing down our necks!'

Parker held Gene's fresh horse steady; his favourite mare, she appeared fractious today. One foot in the stirrup, he had trouble getting into the saddle. Other members of the gang rode out. Parker had his own horse ready and followed them.

Glancing back, he saw that Gene's mare was still acting up, chasing her tail and trying to buck him off. Parker heard him cursing as he was almost thrown, lashing her with his quirt.

Then came a barrage of shots as the posse caught up, and the mare bolted, riderless.

Parker repressed a smile, and urged his horse to a gallop. They kept going through the rain long after the posse had dropped back.

When they reached their hideout, Gene's drinking partner asked, 'What happened back there, Parker? You were the last one away.'

He shrugged. 'I couldn't see clearly — it seemed Gene had trouble controlling his horse.'

One or two regarded him with suspicion, but they couldn't be sure. Parker accepted his share of the loot and waited.

Eventually, a man said, 'We've got to vote on a new leader. Are you in this, Foxy?'

'Why not? If that's what you want.'

Before his eyes closed in sleep that night, Parker thought of Gene for the last time . . . failing to control a mare maddened by the pain of a cactus under the saddle.

★ ★ ★

The scene faded and he was waiting on the plateau with the ghost town behind him. When he heard men and animals coming uphill, he gave a sharp shrill whistle. Immediately, his men came alert, raising their rifles to firing position and covering the opening from the trees.

Two or three young outlaws burst from the greenery, leading mules. They struggled up the final yards, out of breath. One gasped, 'Vigilantes — following us!'

More youngsters arrived, and flung themselves to the ground behind Parker's line of sharpshooters. Nate was one of the last to arrive, his face twisted into a mask of bitterness.

'A trap,' he mumbled, and collapsed. The last of the gang arrived as armed men, miners, came out from the trees.

'All right,' Parker said. 'Let 'em have it. Now!'

Itchy trigger fingers squeezed; rifles cracked and lead flew. For a moment, the miners coming uphill wavered, then came on again, shooting back.

Parker loosed a couple of rounds without aiming; he was not really interested. His men were shooting fast and often, as if this were target practice.

The miners finally realized that they had no cover and little chance of surviving a firefight. A big one yelled, 'Get back to the trees!'

Parker watched them retreat in disorder. Rifle fire continued to shred their covering leaves, driving them further back and down. Some at least must be wounded, and they could only retreat.

'Let them go,' he said, and gave his attention to Nate. 'Where's our gold?'

His challenger looked sullen. 'There isn't any — it was a trap.'

Parker raised an eyebrow. 'So you ran, leading them here?'

'They took us by surprise — '

'You were supposed to take *them* by surprise.' Parker looked over the other young outlaws. 'Anyone hurt? Are you all here?'

'Spike isn't. Figure he caught one.'

Parker frowned at Nate. 'You left the wounded behind?'

'I didn't know,' Nate lied. 'The whole thing was a mess.'

Parker walked away without another word, his expression one of contempt.

An older man sneered, 'So we had to bail you cocksure kids out of trouble.'

Because there was no gold to share out, Nate had lost whatever popularity he might have gained, and the youngsters had lost faith in their rebel leader.

Foxy Parker smiled his sly and secret smile; no one here knew he'd been warned of the trap and had kept that news to himself. He was satisfied that young Nate would not be challenging him again.

* * *

Savage stretched out on his bunk. Doc's parting gift lay in his hand furthest from the grille in the cell door, shielded from view by his body.

It was a thin, flat strip of spring steel, perhaps from a clock, about three inches long and an eighth of an inch wide. It had a well-used appearance, and he could imagine it passing from prisoner to prisoner.

His lip curled back. If Doc had

suspected he was a Pinkerton agent he surely would never have helped him. After dark would be the best time, he decided.

He closed his eyes and rested, dozing lightly. Presently something hard rattled the bars in the door, and he opened his eyes and blinked lazily.

Marshal Kelly stared in at him. 'Hear me. Give my deputy a bad time, I'll give you a hard time.' He turned away. 'I'm off now, Fred.'

'G'night, Marshal.'

Savage waited a few minutes and then peered between the bars at the deputy. He wasn't impressed; Fred was overweight and slovenly, and had a whiskey bottle on the desk. He had already started drinking.

Savage returned to his bunk and pretended to sleep. There was no hurry, and the last thing he wanted was to disturb his guard. He waited, checking the deputy from time to time; the level of the whiskey in the bottle went down steadily.

When he heard a faint snore he moved quickly. Fred had his arms on the desk and his head resting on his arms. He was out.

Savage looked from the window on to the street. It was dark and the only sounds came from a saloon nearby. He studied the lock in the cell door; a standard lock so it should pose no great problem.

He inserted one end of his picklock, and felt for the ward. The metal caught, and he exerted pressure. The worn end of the spring slipped off.

He reversed the pick and started again. It was a matter of feeling, of sensing when the end he couldn't see had engaged. It was not a time for nerves.

The deputy stirred in his sleep and Savage froze. By the time Fred nodded off again, there was sweat on Savage's face and hands.

He dried off his hands on his pants and started again. 'Third time lucky,' he murmured, and felt the end of the pick engage with the ward. He exerted a steady pressure and it moved slowly and then —

Click. The ward snapped back with a surprisingly loud sound. Savage waited, tense. The deputy shifted his position and got his head down again.

Savage eased open the cell door and walked cautiously across the office, passing Fred. The outer door was closed, but not locked, and he stepped outside into the night air.

Breathing deeply of freedom, he moved along the boardwalk to the nearest saloon. Get out of town, he thought, as he looked over the horses hitched to the rail. He chose a big black, loosened the reins and swung into the saddle.

He was heading down Main when the deputy's voice bawled from behind, 'Prisoner loose!'

★　★　★

Beatrice Bottomley struggled to stay calm. She'd managed to persuade the younger children to move back to a safe distance, and some of the women had helped her. But the older boys wanted to be where the fighting was, with Foxy and their fathers.

It was a new experience. She'd believed she was hardened to life in the raw from her childhood spent on a farm; but this Western habit of carrying guns and settling differences with lead was outside the boundaries of her previous life. She began to despair of ever helping these children lead normal lives.

Mary-Ann brought her a bottle. 'Get this down you, Bea.'

'What is it?' She sniffed the pale liquid.

'Brandy, good for shock.'

Bea was not a drinker, but she took the bottle and swallowed. She choked and spluttered, but it warmed her right through and she began to relax.

'It's over now,' Mary-Ann said. 'A nasty trick for Mister Fox to pull, but it seems to have worked.'

Women joined their men again. The outlaws were laughing and joking; some had jugs of whiskey. Children danced around them, but the youngsters of the raiding-party had disappeared; licking their wounds in private, Bea thought.

She looked around. 'Where's Mr Parker?'

Mary-Ann said, 'He went down the hill with a couple of men. He'll make sure they've all gone, and look for Spike. Oh, yes, he's a sly one.'

Bea sat down suddenly. The brandy made her feel better, but her head seemed to be ballooning in and out. 'What d'you mean?'

'Oh, he — '

Mary-Ann broke off, staring towards the hill path. Parker was back, and he didn't look happy.

10

Rope's End

Foxy Parker was feeling pleased with himself as he rode down the track towards the river. He had two gunmen with him, both quicker than most on the trigger, and was not expecting trouble. They were wary, but confident the vigilantes had left. They never got as far as the river.

The man in the lead jerked on the reins and his horse stopped. A body dangled from the branch of a tree, slowly turning; a darkening tongue protruded from the mouth, to show how the young man had died. The corpse smelt, and flies buzzed around it. The second man rolled and lit a cigarette.

Parker froze. Spike! The colour drained from his face as a long-suppressed memory asserted itself, from a time when he was a kid, even younger than Spike . . .

He remembered the heat, the air shimmering in waves. The pool was his secret, small, but deep and hidden in the brush not far from the homestead. He was alone, and had stripped off his clothes and plunged in. Wet. Cool.

He heard a lowing of cattle first, then hoofbeats and men's quiet laughter. He'd been warned: avoid the rancher and his cowboys. His parents had hardly started the homestead when they were warned off. He grabbed his clothes and wriggled deeper into the brush.

Lying flat, he peered through a screen of twigs and leaves. Riders were driving cattle across growing crops. His tiny hands clenched.

Then his father stepped from the house, angry. The rancher on his fine horse laughed.

'You were told to leave, Parker. Now I find my cows on your land . . . that makes you a rustler, and I'm here to show you how we deal with rustlers.'

'I haven't touched your cows — '

A gunshot echoed, and Pa's leg crumpled under him.

A cowboy drawled, 'You can't call a cattleman a liar, sodbuster.'

Ma came running out. 'You've killed him!'

'Not yet . . . '

Young Parker watched in horror, fascinated, as two ropes were tossed over the branch of a tree, each with a noose in it.

One cowboy urged his horse to trample his Pa as he lay on the ground, and Ma screamed, 'You cowards!'

One cowboy dismounted, and went into their log cabin; when he came out, he struck a match and set fire to a bundle of old papers. 'The kid's not here.'

Parker shivered, scared, and burrowed into a mess of old leaves.

'All right, swing 'em. Never mind the kid.'

He heard coarse laughter, and his Ma

sobbing, and covered his eyes.

When he looked out again, the cabin had burnt almost to the ground and the bodies of his parents hung lifeless from the tree. The rancher and his men were riding away, driving their cows before them.

Still he didn't move; it was as if he was frozen inside.

After dark, he began to walk. He walked in the direction of the ranch, till he reached a corral. He helped himself to a horse and rode away. From that moment, he decided, he would take what he wanted . . .

★ ★ ★

His two men were staring at him. He unclenched his hands and took a long, deep breath, forcing his muscles to relax. He turned away from Spike and set off up the hill, muttering to himself. One of the gunmen cut down the body and then he too, followed.

Bea sobered up quickly. One look at Parker's face, contorted in violence, was enough. Men gathered about him, demanding, 'What's up?'

'What's up?' He almost fell out of his saddle. 'I'll tell you what's up! Those bastards lynched a wounded man!'

He was raving like a politician on a soapbox. 'Spike was dead when we cut him down — *choked* to death. They couldn't even hang him properly!'

He spread open his hands, appealing to his audience. 'Haven't I always played the gentleman? Politely requesting their gold and allowing them to live? No more! Vigilantes? By God! I'll show them they've made a *bad* mistake. We'll teach them — '

He ran out of air and paused to gulp more into his lungs. 'They'll get no mercy from me any more — we'll wipe them out!'

Bea stared in amazement. Parker's normal slyness had vanished; he was shaking with emotion, his hands knotted into claws, and his face expressed a viciousness that chilled her. She prayed he would regain his calm before he noticed her.

Mary-Ann shook her grey head. 'Never saw Mister Fox like this before.'

His two gunmen arrived with the body of Spike, and Foxy Parker looked at it with a shudder and turned away.

In that moment, Bea experienced a flash of secret knowledge. The leader of the river pirates had a hidden fear: he lived in dread of death by the rope.

★ ★ ★

'Prisoner loose!'

The shout brought armed drinkers from the saloon, and one of them howled, 'My horse! He's stolen my horse! Get after him!'

The alarm spurred Savage into action. He kicked the black to a gallop, and fled. Beyond the lights of town, night darkness closed in, and he realized he was heading out across open plain — and soon a posse would be at his heels.

The black had powerful legs, but couldn't keep going for ever. This is ridiculous, Savage thought; as a thief in New York, the police had never laid a hand on him, but now, supposed to be on the side of law and order, he had become a hunted man.

He kept riding till he came to a place where the land dipped, and he went down the slope. Moonlight between cloud revealed stacks of logs and tree stumps where a logger had been felling trees. Crazy shadows zigzagged across the whole area.

He reined back and, dismounting, walked his horse in among a jigsaw of shifting shadows. He stroked the animal's muzzle and murmured soothing noises as he waited.

Presently the beating of hoofs echoed, and he held the horse and himself perfectly still and quiet. Riders

134

came at a gallop. He heard Marshal Kelly, far from laconic now his sleep had been ruined, cursing out his deputy. The posse swept by, unable to believe that their quarry could calmly wait among moving shadows while cloud alternately hid and revealed the moon.

Savage smiled tightly as the posse passed beyond sight and hearing. Probably the marshal assumed he would go after the man who'd betrayed him.

He climbed back into the saddle and urged his horse on again, choosing a direction away from the posse's. He recalled the map Winston had shown him of Bottomley's route west. Denver, a town where there would likely be a telegraph office, was his new destination; he intended to send a wire to Allan Pinkerton. It was time to unhorse the new supervisor for the south-west area.

He took it easy during the hours of darkness, resting the black and letting it graze for a while. First light showed Denver on the horizon, and he pushed along a bit faster.

The sky at his back was filling with dark clouds, and he didn't fancy being caught in the open in a downpour. He approached the town by following the iron rails to the depot and saw, immediately opposite, the telegraph office.

He hitched the black and, as he walked to the door, glanced through the office window. A man was standing at the counter, talking to the key operator; a man he recognized from the past and was surprised to see again.

Dave Bridger, a New York detective, had been the temporary supervisor at Pinkerton's Fremont office, and was supposed to be back in New York.

When he walked into the office, Bridger exclaimed, 'Savage! What the hell are you doing here? You're a long way out of your area.'

'Figured to send Mr Allan a wire.'

'No need for that,' Bridger said

brusquely. 'Mr Allan has given new orders that apply to all of us. Drop all routine enquiries to find the man who killed Winston!'

11

False Identity

The man who'd been calling himself Winston was sick of driving his hired buggy across what seemed to be a plain with no end. He was sick of the American West and roughing it, and wanted to get back to civilized life.

Soon now, he thought. Savage was safely in jail. He knew where Bottomley was. The masquerade was over, and he could take direct action. It was the first time he'd had to feed and water horses, the first time he hadn't hired helpers to take care of the many practical details, but he didn't know anyone he could trust in this country. So there'd been problems, and he'd overcome them.

He squinted into the distance. Through a heat haze buildings loomed, with hills behind them, and his spirits rose. This had to be the crosstrails store Savage had mentioned; he could rest a while before going up.

The store grew in size and number of outbuildings as he neared; and the signboard — MARRIAGES PERFORMED : BURIALS ARRANGED — amused him. He decided he might get on well with Chandler.

He stopped beside the main entrance, stepped down, and brushed the dust from his coat.

A lanky man dressed like a cowboy sat on a fence, whittling a piece of wood. He called out, 'Feed and water your horses, two bucks.'

He felt in his pocket for a couple of coins and tossed them into a brown hand. Why not? He was still using the balance of the money he'd taken from the office safe in Fremont.

He walked inside and up to a counter, ignoring the cornucopia of goods for sale, advertisements, and the men seated at tables.

'I'll have a meal,' he said, 'with a

bottle of wine and a cigar.'

Chandler looked into pale blue eyes. 'You will, will you? That'll be five dollars in advance.' He held out a weatherbeaten hand covered with fading tattoos.

'I've heard there's a man named Parker up there in an old mining town. Is that right?'

'Information's extra.'

'Of course it is, old boy. Anything else I need will cost extra too, I've no doubt. If you've a backroom, let's step in there for a private chat. I don't want everyone to know my business. It'll be worth your while, I assure you.

'English?' Chandler asked. 'Maybe looking for an English teacher, like the one before yuh?'

He smiled at this mention of Savage, and how easy he'd been to fool. 'In private.'

'Of course, Mr — ? I didn't get your name.'

'Gardiner.'

The storekeeper lifted a flap to allow

him behind the counter, and then opened a door leading into a small storeroom filled from floor to ceiling with cartons. He closed the door behind him.

'Waal, what is it you want, Mr Gardiner?'

Gardiner opened his wallet and brought out a sheaf of notes, divided them neatly and gave Chandler a third. It took only a short while to reach an agreement and by then his meal was ready.

'Best if you stay overnight,' Chandler said. 'It's not an easy trail in the dark. In the morning, I'll provide a mule to get you up there.'

* * *

'Winston's dead?'

Savage stared at Bridger in astonishment. 'What happened?'

'Shot with a .41 revolver.'

Savage found it hard to believe. 'When? Where? He told the Cheyenne marshal I wasn't a Pinkerton, and I've only just got out of jail.'

'Cheyenne? You're not making sense — '

Bridger gave a snort and broke off. 'Let's go for breakfast and sort this out over a meal.'

'Suits me. I'm missing a meal, and I'm broke.'

The Railroad Hotel, where Bridger had booked a room, was a brick building with single rooms upstairs and one large dining-room below. It catered for transients, and breakfast was standard and basic: bacon and eggs with hash browns, beans and as much coffee as they could drink.

While they waited for service, Bridger listened to Savage's version of events with amazement.

'The man calling himself Winston sent you to find this teacher? Why?'

Savage shrugged. 'All he said was a client was paying us to find her.'

'Garbage,' Bridger snapped. 'This is the first I've heard of the woman, and

I've come straight from our New York office. I wish I hadn't been in such a hurry to get away when he took over from me at Fremont. If I'd insisted on a more detailed takeover, I might have smelt a rat.'

Their food arrived and Bridger paused for a moment.

'But that's water under the bridge — and I'm not happy about being sent west again. I simply did not imagine he wasn't the real Winston.'

Savage's fork, loaded with bacon, became motionless half-way to his mouth. 'He wasn't? He fooled me.'

'He fooled a lot of people. He got away with the impersonation because when he killed our new supervisor on the way to Fremont — outside Kansas City — he removed his clothes so it took a while to identify the body.'

Savage had difficulty taking it in. He spoke slowly. 'So I was taking orders from Winston's killer?' He'd been tricked and didn't like it — and he'd ended up in jail. A cold anger began to build in him. 'Do we know his real name?'

'Not so far. Head office is in touch with the English police.'

The bacon Savage was chewing had lost its flavour, and he pushed his plate away.

'Mr Allan is warning all agents. We simply can't allow him, whoever he is, to get away with this. We'd be laughed out of the business. We must find him and deal with him ourselves.'

Savage bared his teeth. 'Got the same idea myself. What do we do about the teacher?'

'Forget her. She doesn't come into this — except this killer used us to find her for reasons of his own.'

'What reasons?'

Bridger looked blank, then called for more coffee. 'Who cares? Concentrate on Winston's killer, whatever his damn name is.'

'I need outfitting,' Savage said. 'What I had was taken by Parker's men, and I've a borrowed horse to get rid of. I need a shotgun and ammo, a knife and spending money.'

Dave Gridger shuddered. 'This business is going to cost the agency a fortune, with no client to foot the bill. And you can bet the false Winston cleaned out the office safe before he quit Fremont.'

He emptied his coffee cup and stood up.

'I'll turn your horse over to the marshal here, and he can explain to the law in Cheyenne. I'll need a horse, too. Reckon he'll head for that ghost town?'

'He wants the teacher for some reason — remember, they're both English — so wherever Bottomley is, I'm betting we'll find our killer.'

They left the hotel, and by midday were outfitted and on the trail, all in time to watch the sun disappear behind billowing dark clouds.

★ ★ ★

Foxy Parker had control of himself again. The old fear that had surfaced was, once more, locked away in a corner of his brain. He waited at the top of the hill, watching the trail where it left the trees. The light was poor, the clouds low.

'One man, calling himself Gardiner, riding a mule,' had been the message from Chandler's man, 'looking for a schoolteacher.'

Beside him, Mary-Ann growled like a bear whose hibernation had been disturbed. 'No one's getting Bea — she's too valuable.'

Parker thought she must be right. First Savage, and now Gardiner. He was puzzled because he couldn't see what made the English woman so important. But he could smell profit in the situation, so he waited patiently; with a couple of sharpshooters hidden from sight.

He heard a slow clip-clop of hoofs, and a figure came into view; a mule carrying a man in a city suit, with a neatly trimmed moustache. He sat awkwardly in the saddle as he covered the last dusty patch, and halted, looking around as calmly as a tourist visiting a beauty spot, studying the layout of the buildings and sparing a glance towards him.

Finally he lit a cigar and drew on it, climbed down from the mule and walked towards them, his gaze mostly on Mary-Ann.

'Looking for someone?' Parker challenged.

Gardiner shifted his attention. 'You must be Parker. I'm looking for Miss Beatrice Bottomley. Is she here?'

Parker noticed the accent. 'English?'

'Yes indeed, old boy, as English as Miss Bottomley. I've come all the way from England to claim her.'

He smiled, and Parker recognized the type; a woman-charmer.

'You paid Savage to find her?'

'I ordered him to find her.'

'Where is he now?'

Gardiner laughed out loud and

waved his cigar in the air. 'In jail, in Cheyenne.'

Parker frowned him down. 'So why come all this way after a schoolteacher?'

Gardiner removed his hat and bowed to Mary-Ann. 'For love, Mr Parker, for the great romance of my life. I wish to propose marriage.'

Mary-Ann gave a snort of disbelief. 'So you say!'

Parker turned to her. 'Where is she now?'

'In school, of course.' She regarded the Englishman as she would a rattlesnake.

'Fetch her,' said Parker.

'Can't this wait, Mister Fox?'

He shook his head. 'I need to know what's going on.'

Grumbling, Mary-Ann strode towards the school hut. Gardiner watched which building she entered, and hummed a few bars of 'Oh! Susanna'.

Parker touched the butt of his revolver as he waited. Was the man a fool? Did he really think he could just ride into the Fox's town, and ride out again?

Bea came from the school class, with Mary-Ann, and walked towards them. Gardiner bowed, giving the smile that had moved the heart of many a woman.

'My dear Beatrice,' he drawled, 'it is a great pleasure at last to — '

'Who are you?' she asked bluntly. 'You're interrupting a class.'

Parker said, 'He's told us he's come from England to marry you. How about that?'

Bea stared blankly. 'I've never seen him before in my life!'

12

Night Stalk

A silence developed after Bea Bottomley's denial, and was broken when a man laughed.

Parker tipped back his sombrero. 'What d'yuh say to that, Mr Gardiner?'

The Englishman remained relaxed, giving the impression that he didn't have a worry in the world. He drew on his cigar, and his words came out smooth and slick as oil.

'It's true we've never been introduced, and Bea may not have noticed me in the background, but I assure you I have admired my love from a distance, longing only for an excuse to approach. Now I can — '

Mary-Ann snorted. 'What a horse's arse! Kill him quick, the way you would a snake.'

Parker kept his gaze fixed on Gardiner's face, which was hard to read, but he never doubted Mary-Ann was right. What game was this Englishman playing? He still scented a profit, and was reluctant to lose an opportunity.

Bea asked, 'Is that all, Mr Parker?'

'For now.'

She turned away and walked towards the schoolhouse as men crowded around Gardiner.

'Search him,' Parker said.

Eager hands turned out his pockets. They found no weapons, not even a penknife.

Mad, Parker thought, coming here unarmed.

Then a man shouted, 'Look!' and held up a solid gold ring.

So maybe he means it? Parker thought. He was still deliberating when the grey gloom darkened and he looked up. Clouds were sinking and closing in like a curtain to shroud the hilltop.

When Bea turned away she was

feeling uneasy. First Mr Savage, now this man Gardiner, looking for her. Why should they seek her out here? She couldn't grasp what was going on.

To add to her confusion, Oscar suddenly stepped in front of her. She recognized him because he was older and looked half-way respectable; he was the one who'd taken her off the boat, and brought her trunk from Cheyenne. Somehow she didn't feel threatened by him, and was struck by the fact he was freshly shaven, his suit brushed, and he was holding his hat in his hand.

'Miss Beatrice, I only want to say you can rely on me. I admire yuh, and if you feel the need, can offer you my protection — '

She was stunned. Oscar, in his own way, was courting her! Inspired by Gardiner, no doubt; so how long would it be before other members of the gang got ideas? She shivered, and then her lips firmed.

It was time to make herself clear; the children came first, that was what was important. Mary-Ann would stand by her . . . wouldn't she?

'Thank you for your offer, sir, but I'm a teacher and intend to remain one.'

Thunder rolled, the storm broke with forked lightning, and rain bucketed down. They ran for cover.

★　★　★

Rain had already started to fall when Savage and Dave Bridger reached Chandler's cross trails store; big, fat, warm drops. By the time they'd stabled their horses, a mass of grey cloud hid the top of the hills, and wind-driven rain lashed them as they ran for the main building.

Savage pushed inside and Bridger slammed the door and leaned against it. They got their breath back and huddled around the pot-bellied iron stove. Chandler called, 'Help you, gents?'

'Yeah,' Bridger growled. 'Whiskey, and leave the bottle.'

'Coffee, hot, and plenty of it.'

Savage picked a table close to the stove and away from the few other travellers. Talk died, and they sat listening to rain hammering on the tin roof. The man dressed as a cowboy got up and lit an oil lamp.

Chandler came from behind the counter with a bottle and glass, and a large mug filled with coffee. He looked directly at Savage.

'Seem to recall your face . . . paid Foxy a visit, didn't yuh? Did you ever see that English teacher you were after?'

'I saw her.'

Chandler nodded towards Bridger. 'Who's your friend? Is he looking for her, too?'

Bridger poured himself a whiskey. 'It's an Englishman I'm after. Wears a city suit, fair hair and moustache, smokes cigars. Have you seen anyone like that?'

'Maybe.' Chandler appeared to be giving the matter serious thought, and

Savage placed two dollar coins on the table.

'Fellah answering to your description called here, then went up the hill ahead of the storm. Like you, he was interested in the teacher woman. Thinking of following him?'

'Guess I might,' Savage admitted. 'But not till the rain stops.'

Chandler nodded. 'You may not find it so easy to get away next time. I heard Foxy was real put out about that.'

Savage shrugged. 'So? I'm hungry — let's have something to eat.'

'I've got pork chops — '

'They'll do.'

'Me too,' Bridger added.

After Chandler had gone behind his counter, Savage said quietly, 'It'll be best if you stay here and keep an eye on our host — I'm not inclined to trust him further than I can see him. It'll be a case of watch my back while I go after Winston.'

'You're going up alone?'

'On foot, under cover of the rain.

Parker won't be expecting visitors in this weather.'

When their meal came, Savage said, 'We'll book a room with two beds. I'm about all in.'

Bridger said, 'Guess I'll stay a while to finish this bottle.'

'Please yourselves — just so long as you pay me,' said Chandler.

Savage finished his meal and pushed the empty plate aside.

'How'll you get back down?' Bridger asked.

Savage bared his teeth. 'Foxy owes me a horse from before.' He got up and went towards the door.

'Take the first shack on the left past the stable,' Chandler called after him, and Savage nodded and went out into the rain. He dropped his gear in the hut Chandler had indicated, then moved quickly towards the trees.

Before he reached their cover, he was soaked to the skin. He waited beneath a pine tree, trying to see through a curtain of rain that reminded him of a waterfall. Only when lightning flashed could he make out the trail leading upwards. He could hear only between peals of thunder, and what he heard was water gushing downhill as if overflowing from a drainpipe. Obviously no one could see or hear him, either.

It had never been like this in New York, he thought. There had always been a doorway to dodge into, an empty warehouse or covered arcade linking two streets. Here there were only trees, and their leaves leaked water; large drops splashed as they fell on him.

He waited for the next flash before he went on up, a knife at his waist, empty shotgun in his hand. He had shells in his pocket, but they probably wouldn't fire anyway; but ramming the muzzle into a man's stomach might frighten him to death.

It was dark beneath the trees. Underfoot, wet leaves and mud made the ground slippery, and more than once he slid backwards. Water ran down the trail and, at times, he felt as though he were wading through a stream.

The storm raged; thunder echoed like a barrage of heavy guns, and lightning dazzled. Water sluiced down as if the heavens had an unending supply.

When he reached the edge of the trees, he stood quietly, watching the open ground, trying to detect a sentry. Nothing moved except branches in the wind. The only sound was that of rain beating down.

Parker wouldn't be pleased if his guard was holed up in the dry somewhere. He listened, and stared into the shadows. The downpour drowned all human sounds.

Then he glimpsed a small red glow; a man cupping his hands around a cigarette. He moved past him, and studied the open ground he had to cover. There didn't appear to be another man on watch.

He was reasonably sure he'd reached

the ghost town undetected, so where was Winston? The fake supervisor had made a fool of him, and he wanted revenge — and if Foxy Parker got in his way, he'd pay him back for caging him. He considered Mary-Ann; did he want a return match? Savage decided not — but he remembered the large gold nugget he'd seen in her hut. There must be a lot of gold squirrelled away here somewhere.

The English woman? She'd given him water when he was desperate, and released him from the cage. He felt tempted to warn her, but frowned and told himself he owed nobody anything.

Concentrate; straight in, deal with Winston, grab any gold lying around, and leave.

He waited for the next gust of wind to drive straight at the group of huts, and then scurried across the plateau among the debris which had been picked up and carried along by the storm. His immediate target was a window where the yellow light of an oil lamp glowed.

He reached the wooden wall and edged close to an uncurtained window. He heard a voice and peered in. He'd found the schoolma'am, reading aloud to a bunch of kids.

He moved around the side of the hut to the porch. This gave him brief shelter from the wind and rain, and enabled him to get his breath back.

Water dripped from his nose, and he wiped his face with a sleeve. Likely she'd know where Winston was. He tapped gently on the door and waited, tapped again. The door opened a fraction.

'Who's there?'

He kept out of the light escaping past the door, his voice low. 'Savage.'

The door opened wider and he saw surprise on her face. 'Why have you come back? Mr Parker will — '

He cut in: 'Where's Winston?'

Her blank expression told him the man was using another name. 'The Englishman.'

'Oh, you mean Mr Gardiner?' she said.

'Is that what he's calling himself? Be careful of him — he's a killer.'

'Aren't you all?' she replied sadly. 'I suppose he's with Mr Parker.'

Savage hesitated before he turned away. He gestured at the heavy rain, the gloom.

'Now's your chance to get away. There's a store at the bottom of the hill, and Dave Bridger's there. He's a Pinkerton, and he'll help you.'

She looked puzzled. 'A Pinkerton?'

'A detective, from New York. Now, where can I find Parker?'

'I can't leave the children. They need me — '

He saw her eyes widen as she looked past him, and started to turn. He glimpsed a shadowy figure and then something hard smashed against his skull. The pain overwhelmed him before he hit the ground.

13

Wealth is Relative

Someone was shaking him. Muffled voices he could hear seemed a long way off. His head throbbed and, when he tried to move, a sudden sharp pain stabbed him. Perhaps he groaned. He opened his eyes, which seemed gummed together, and daylight made him blink. Was it morning already? Memory cut in; the storm was over.

A voice, closer now; someone leaning over him. A voice filled with satisfaction. 'Your luck's run out, Mr Savage. Bottomley won't be releasing you this time around.'

Parker's voice. He'd come up the hill, in the rain, to get Winston's killer, and had been talking to the teacher when —

He came alert. He was lying on bare boards, just inside a long wooden hut with the door open. His wrists were tied together in front of him, and his ankles hobbled. He looked up.

Foxy Parker had a pleased expression. Bottomley appeared anxious. Winston — no, Gardiner — was smoking a cigar. Mary-Ann watched the Englishman with a sour expression on her face and a meat cleaver in her hand. Remembering the gold nugget in her hut, Savage tried a smile on her. No reaction.

Parker said, 'I think Oscar overdid it. Maybe he hasn't forgiven you for following him here — but, you'll live, for the moment.'

His ugly face showed cunning; he was obviously pleased to have two prisoners, to play one against the other. Savage glanced at Bea. She was a fool not to have taken her chance to get away; he hoped she had enough sense to keep quiet about Dave Bridger, waiting below at the crosstrails store.

Gardiner said coldly, 'I advise killing Savage now. He's a Pinkerton, and has a reputation for getting out of tight places.'

'Time enough for that,' Parker said. 'Maybe he'll help provide an answer to the question: why is an English woman who teaches kids worth all this bother?'

That was something Savage would like to know, too.

'It was Gardiner, or whatever his name is, who hired me to find her. So what's he after? He's the only one who knows.'

'Mr Gardiner,' Parker purred, 'perhaps you'd care to answer that question. I'm sure we'd all like to know, and you do seem to be the one who started the chase.'

The Englishman smiled, and concentrated on enjoying his cigar.

Parker waited, then added, 'Why make it difficult for yourself?'

He sighed. 'That you travelled from your own country for the love of a woman is romantic, but doesn't ring true to me.'

Mary-Ann impatiently lifted her meat

cleaver. 'Let me chop a few bits off'n him, Mister Fox. I'll guarantee to loosen his tongue.'

Gardiner said hastily, 'There's no need for unpleasantness. Of course there's money involved, quite a lot of it, so I'm sure we can do a deal.'

He paused. 'Money, and property. Miss Bottomley is a very rich woman. A distant relative died and left a fortune — and the only other close relative had died just previously. It took time for the family lawyers to trace her, and before they succeeded, she'd left the country.'

Bea's mouth opened, but no sound came out.

'So she is now a wealthy heiress who owns a large country house, with servants, and has substantial funds awaiting her in a bank.'

Parker smirked. 'And when you marry her, you'll get your hands on the money. *That* I can understand.'

'Well, I can't,' Bea said. 'I don't know of any rich relatives. Why should I believe you? You've told lies before and, anyway, I don't want a big house with servants. I like teaching.'

Parker rubbed the side of his nose. 'It needs thinking about — obviously Bea is too valuable to be allowed to leave us.' He turned to a couple of his men. 'Put the Englishman in the cage for now.'

Gardiner protested, 'You need me, Parker — I know the law back home. We can — '

Parker's men ignored his words and hustled him away. Savage watched with approval as he was locked in; he knew where to find him once he freed himself.

Parker regarded him coldly. 'I've other plans for you, Mr Savage.'

* * *

Dave Bridger yawned. He sat in Chandler's store, nursing an almost empty bottle, and supposed he must have dozed off. He became aware that the storm had died, and briefly considered walking to the shack they'd paid for and stretching out on a bed.

But, like Savage, he didn't have a lot of trust in this storekeeper. Savage must have got to the top of the hill in his hunt for Winston's killer, and he wondered what was happening up there.

Not that he worried about the kid he'd taken off the New York waterfront. Savage had proved himself to be a survivor more than once; when he went up against the Preacher's gang and, later, against the Howard clan.

He was tough, and Bridger could easily believe Savage would come out on top over any odds; but that didn't mean he had to trust him. He had the feeling Savage would go along with any Pinkerton job, all the while looking out for himself.

It was strange how Savage had adapted to this way of life; he hated it. The heat got him down and the food upset his stomach; since coming West he'd learnt to appreciate his sister's cooking. He felt uneasy in the wild; but city crooks he understood and could cope with.

But suppose Savage was wrong about the killer being after the schoolma'am? Where should they start looking then? All that mattered was nailing Winston's murderer, so he could get back East.

He poured the last of the whiskey and sipped it, listening to the quiet calling of the card-players in the corner. 'Pass . . . buy one . . . twenty-one.' Chandler was slumped behind his counter.

The door opened and a man came in. Bridger noted the thick whiskers hiding most of the face, and his hard-worn overalls and heavy boots; a miner, he guessed.

The newcomer went directly to Chandler but, before the stranger could speak, the storekeeper cautioned him to silence and opened a flap in the counter. They both disappeared into a room at the back.

Interesting, but there was nothing

Bridger could do about it with the card-players in the room. When Chandler returned, Bridger called for a fresh bottle and invited the newcomer to drink with him.

'Come far?' he asked.

'Far enough. And I'll take a drink with anyone, stranger.'

'How's the travelling now?'

'If you're thinking of moving on, I'd wait for the ground to dry out.'

'Are there many mines around here?'

'Some.' The man waved a hand in the direction of the hills.

Bridger discovered that the man opened his mouth easily enough to pour whiskey in, but few words came out. He gave it up.

Chandler wrote something on a sheet of paper, folded it, and sealed it with hot wax. He crossed the room and handed the note to one of the card-players.

The lanky man dressed as a cowboy chucked his cards on the table and stood up. 'I'll take my revenge another time,' he said, and went outside.

Bridger heard a horse leave, and wondered: what was that all about?

* * *

Shepherd rode easy in the saddle as he set off up the hill to the old mining village. He sang quietly a few verses of 'Bury Me Not on the Lone Prairie', and his horse didn't object. In his imagination he was riding around a herd of cattle.

Shepherd dressed like a cowboy because he'd always wanted to be one, and liked other people to believe he was. He wore a flannel shirt, and chaps over denim pants; a neckerchief at his throat and Stetson on his head; cowboy boots with rounded spurs, a coiled lariat and a holstered Colt .45; all supplied by his boss.

He lived a rich fantasy life in his head, and practised his shooting every day.

For one month, in his green days,

he'd tried the life, but other cowhands treated him as a figure of fun. 'Baa!' they would bleat; or 'Have you lost your flock?'; and 'How much wool can we get from a longhorn?' It wore him down. Some men might have changed their name, but he chose to quit and ride on; after all, he'd tried the life of a cowhand long enough to learn it was hard work for long hours and small pay.

By comparison, his job at Chandler's store was not demanding, and it was easier to pretend; most travellers assumed he was a cowboy between jobs, so why sweat at the real thing?

Sometimes he carried messages up the hill to Parker, who could be generous when he was in a good mood. Shepherd reached the top of the track and looked about for Foxy.

★ ★ ★

Beyond Parker, Savage saw the lanky cowboy from Chandler's ride from the trees towards them. The messenger dismounted and said, 'Something for yuh, Foxy.'

Parker turned and held his hand out for the note, and fumbled some coins from his pocket. Another man gave the cowboy a bottle and he took a drink.

Savage, still lying on bare boards, watched Parker break the seal; he looked excited and avarice showed in his eyes. He stepped outside the hut and lifted his voice.

'Good news, boys — listen to this. 'The next boat upriver will be the real McCoy. Some miners who didn't carry gold last time, will be carrying extra. The boat is leaving on the — ' '

Parker's men gathered quickly, eager for details. Savage recognized Nate and Oscar, the two look-outs; he saw Mary-Ann and Bea in the background.

For the moment, no one was watching him, and he tried the cords holding him; they were tight, but if he had time alone, he could reach his ankles. He flexed his fingers . . .

He was not one to give up, but his

head still throbbed and he wasn't thinking clearly.

He saw Parker's face change. Before it had registered greed; now it darkened with anger, and he crumpled the note and threw it to the ground.

'It's the *New Victoria* again, those bastards, the ones who hanged a wounded man, the scum who murdered Spike! They've got a nerve using our river again — '

Parker's face was pale with tension, his hands clenching and unclenching, his legs shifting position as if he couldn't stand still.

Men began to edge away from their leader. Mary-Ann gripped Bea's arm, urging her to leave. The cowboy mounted his horse, turned its head and rode back down the hill.

'We'll have to teach these self-appointed vigilantes a lesson.' Parker's eyes glinted. 'Teach them they can't get away with murder!'

This was a new side to Parker revealed, the man's face made even uglier by viciousness. He trembled with suppressed fury. Unstable, Savage thought confidently; once he was free he could easily deal with him.

Parker was still raving. 'We'll show no mercy. We'll wreck their boat, wipe out everyone — crew and miners, taking everything they've got.'

He had to pause to take a breath. 'We'll show them how we deal with treachery. We'll butcher them!'

His gaze settled on Savage, and he strode towards him. 'You, too, spy. We'll take you with us, and I personally will put a bullet in you. You'll just be one more body . . . perhaps someone will think you're an outlaw killed in the raid!'

He lashed out with his boot and Savage wriggled sideways to dodge the full weight of it.

14

River Ambush

Savage heard Parker laugh and saw him walk off, shouting orders.

'I want every man on this raid.' He was calming down, all business now. 'We'll need extra ammunition, axes, kerosene. Bring the Pinkerton spy, too.'

Oscar cut the hobble about Savage's ankles and forced him to walk to a mule, then heaved him into the saddle. Savage clung on while his ankles were tied together beneath the mule.

Savage sat, waiting. Outlaws scurried to get guns and canvas sacks; he saw Nate, with other youngsters, join the men. Then Oscar prodded the mule into motion and he joined the cavalcade jogging down towards the river to intercept the *New Victoria*.

Savage quickly realized this was a

different trail from the one leading to Chandler's store. The raiders rode in silence, and he suspected that some of them felt uneasy over their leader's outburst.

He spoke to a horseman beside him. 'You reckon Foxy's crazy?'

'Shut your mouth!'

Savage smiled; he'd always found the sowing of dissension among the enemy a sound policy. 'I wonder how many of you the vigilantes will hang this time?'

The rider lifted his quirt and lashed him. 'Shut up!'

Savage laughed. 'Feeling nervous, are you?'

Nate was riding just ahead, close by Parker. He asked, 'You heading for the place where they ambushed me?'

'That's right, Nate. The one place they won't be expecting us. We'll surprise them, because they'll be too cocky to believe we might attack here a second time.'

Half-way down the slope the trees began to thin out, leaving open ground.

Parker reined back and gave the order, 'Load the mules with dry brushwood.'

His men were puzzled, but obeyed: obviously they hadn't done this before. Only Nate was bold enough to ask, 'Why?'

Parker's sly smile returned. 'It's all part of the surprise . . . '

Mules loaded, they continued down towards the river. Savage heard water running before he glimpsed it; the track wound between stands of leafy trees until it reached a bank and a projecting spit of land.

At this point the river was wide but shallow, and the only deep channel lay close to the bank, where the raiders stopped; an ideal place for an ambush.

Oscar cut Savage's ankle ropes and pushed him out of the saddle to the ground. Another rope was used to hobble him, and he was tied to a tree to stop him wandering.

Parker began placing his men. He directed two axemen to begin felling a large tree, and ordered the brushwood to be piled into a small boat moored close by.

When he was satisfied with his preparations, he looked towards his prisoner. 'Not long to go, Mr Savage, if you're the praying kind.'

Savage's lip curled. 'Not me, Mr Parker. You're the one who's going to swing at the end of a rope — '

Parker swore and screamed abuse. For a moment, he lost control again, and his men exchanged worried glances.

* * *

Bea Bottomley watched the last of the outlaws vanish among the trees on the trail down to the river, and began to herd the children into the schoolroom. She hadn't tried before, because she'd known it would have been a waste of energy.

Mary-Ann had retired to her own hut, and the other women had gone off chatting amongst themselves.

Bea faced two rows of small, overexcited faces and realized she wouldn't be able to concentrate on a lesson; even here she sensed an air of violence. She couldn't help Mr Savage, but there was still the other prisoner.

Gardiner was locked in the miners' cage, and possibly she could free him.

She picked out the freckle-faced boy who wanted to read. 'Luke, you're in charge of the class while I'm away. I shall only be a few minutes, so keep order, please, till I come back.'

'Yes, Miss Beatrice.'

Outside, the plateau was deserted except for a small black-and-white dog that followed her to the big wheel that suspended the cage over the old mine shaft. She seized the handle of the ratchet and swung the cage away from the hole in the ground.

Gardiner watched her without speaking. Bottomley released the rope, and the cage settled on the ground. Immediately she pulled a pin from her hair and went to work on the padlock.

When the door swung open, Gardiner stepped out.

Bea said, 'You'd best leave quickly while you can. I don't know how soon Mr Parker will arrive back.'

Gardiner glared at her. He was annoyed at having been caged, and then forgotten about when the outlaws had left their town.

'Don't tell me what to do!' The dog growled and he kicked it and walked off. He'd made a note of where Parker's men had left the mule Chandler had provided.

He reached under the saddle for the small derringer he'd hidden there. He put the gun in his pocket and felt on top again. A length of rope caught his eye and he picked it up; things were going his way again.

Humming, he led the mule back to where Bea waited. 'We'll go down to the store, Beatrice, where Mr Chandler will — '

'I advise you to go now,' she said calmly. 'I'm staying here.'

He shook his head and laughed. 'I don't think so.' From the corner of his eye, he glimpsed movement. Someone was approaching: the tough-looking woman, with a meat cleaver in her hand.

Bea urged, 'Go now. Hurry!'

Gardiner ignored her. He half-turned to face Mary-Ann, and waited till she was almost within touching distance, then made a lightning draw and squeezed the trigger. The bullet struck her full in the chest, driving her backwards. A red stain spread across her shirt, and she gave a little grunt and collapsed.

Bea stared in horror, stunned by the swiftness of his actions. 'Oh, no!' She dropped to her knees beside Mary-Ann. Blood was pumping from a large hole in her chest, the light already fading from her eyes.

'You — murderer!' she cried.

She got to her feet and faced Gardiner. He reloaded, and holstered his gun inside his coat, then struck

Bea across the face.

'That's no way to speak to your husband. I can see I'll need to teach you obedience.'

Bea staggered, too shocked to grasp his meaning. He looped one end of the rope around her wrists, and tied the other end to the mule. He climbed into the saddle and set off downhill. Bea stumbled along behind as the rope tightened.

★ ★ ★

Savage's smile was cruel as he watched Parker struggle to control himself. The outlaws were watching their leader, and he enjoyed undermining their trust in him.

Parker stalked away to the two axemen cutting away at the base of a tree trunk. 'Enough, wait now.' He told the man with the kerosene can to stand by.

The rest of the gang settled down, screened by leafy branches overhanging

182

the water. Savage worked on his knots when no one was looking; it was a slow business, and insects tormented him. The damp heat made him drowsy; to rouse himself he imagined Gardiner imprisoned in his cage.

Presently he heard a rhythmic *thump-thump* of a steam engine, and snapped alert.

A dark cloud rose above the cottonwoods and then he glimpsed smokestacks; seconds later, the *New Victoria* swept into view. She swung through an arc, moving in close to the river-bank to take advantage of the deep water channel.

He could see miners crowding the deck, and firemen throwing logs into the furnace; obviously the captain wanted maximum speed to get past this danger spot. Savage concentrated on freeing himself; he knew a shouted warning would never be heard above the noise of the engine.

Parker gave a shrill whistle. The pair of loggers swung their axes to remove the last of the wood holding up the tree; it swayed, toppled towards the water, and fell with a crash across the bow of the steamboat. Miners screamed as they tried to avoid the heavy tree trunk.

The captain bawled, 'More steam — faster — keep going!'

Parker shouted at his man with the kerosene can: 'Now!'

The outlaw tipped the can so that oil ran out, splashing over the brushwood in the small boat. Parker cut the mooring rope, struck a match and tossed it on the oil. The kerosene flared up immediately, then the brushwood caught fire. Parker used a pole to push the burning boat towards the steamer.

A voice on the *New Victoria* cried out: '*Fireship!*'

Some miners struggled to reach the far side of the boat, and the steamer tilted; the crew panicked, and one or two men jumped overboard.

From the wheelhouse, a voice shouted, 'Reverse engines,' and the giant paddlewheel at the stern slowed to a stop. By now the steamer was beginning to burn; flames crackled and oily smoke billowed. The *New Victoria* wallowed out of control; the current caught it, and carried it on to a sandbank, where it stuck fast.

Foxy Parker shouted: 'Boarders, no mercy!'

Savage had freed his ankles and was working on his wrists when Parker turned to him, grinning. 'Your turn!' A revolver barrel slammed down on his head, hard enough to daze him.

Parker sliced the remaining cords, stuck a knife in Savage's belt, and pulled him upright. Savage staggered as a shotgun was pushed into his hands.

The outlaws swarmed aboard the steamer, firing into the crowd. Parker shoved Savage in front of him on to the boat, levelled his revolver, and shot him from behind. Savage sprawled, face down, on the deck.

15

Widowmaker

The rope cut into her wrists and the movement of the mule kept her off balance. She was jerked painfully along, like a puppet on a string, and several times almost fell.

Gardiner sat easy in the saddle, giving an impression of an English gentleman finding everything right with the world. Not quite right; Parker's men had taken his wallet and cigars; but soon to be put right. The mule ignored both of them.

Bea thought sadly of Mary-Ann lying still and cold in the dirt, and blamed herself for that, and of the kids she'd left in Luke's charge. She could hardly believe she was being dragged downhill at the end of a rope. Did Gardiner really intend to marry her? Could he really believe she was wealthy? Why else would he bother with her?

Bea Bottomley was confused. Her world had turned upside-down, but now she was coming out of the shock and getting angry. There had been no need to kill Mary-Ann, and she despised Gardiner for that. Her chin set obstinately. If he believed she was going to submit willingly, he was wrong; he'd have a fight on his hands.

She stumbled and slid down the muddy slope, finding it difficult to keep her balance with her arms stretched out in front of her. A branch lashed her face, drawing blood.

The words of Mr Savage jogged her memory: 'He's a killer.' She should have taken more notice. Too late now, but what else had he said? 'A store at the bottom of the hill, and Dave Bridger's there'. Some kind of detective, it seemed. Perhaps he would help her?

Gardiner, she decided, must be stupid, tying himself to a woman who despised him, just to get his hands on money. Assuming he was serious. She would refuse to marry him, of course; but would she have that choice?

She remembered why she'd left England, after her parents died, and a chill edged along her spine; there hadn't been much choice at Cromwell's Private Academy. She hadn't thought of her past for a while; life here had been one excitement after another, but now all the memories came flooding back.

Mr Cromwell, small, bald and spiteful, ran his school for unwanted children with the maxim: 'Minimum board, maximum punishment'. Mrs Cromwell, gross, simpering and always helping herself to food intended for the children, would murmur, 'Just testing, Cromwell. This food is much too good to waste on such reluctant pupils.'

'Just so, my dear. We must take care they don't put on weight — most unhealthy.'

Teaching at Cromwell's, her first job

after leaving the farm, had come as a shock.

Only the new children cried; they learnt quickly that tears brought a caning, that almost any behaviour brought a beating. They became silent, sullen and scared. How could parents dump their children in a place like this? she wondered. Unwanted children put out of the way under the pretence of educating them.

'Spare the rod and spoil the child,' chanted Mr Cromwell, enthusiastically beating a boy who had answered back.

It had disturbed Bea when she received orders: 'Don't waste time trying to teach these ungrateful brats. Call them obstinate and thrash them. Obedience is the main lesson here, and they'll learn that quicker if you take the skin off them!'

I'm not a teacher, Beatrice had thought glumly, more of a prison warder. Sometimes it felt as if the Cromwells owned her outright, and that *she* was as much a prisoner as the children.

'Silence is golden' was one rule, along with 'Children should be seen, but not heard', including those times when they were needed for unpaid work around the building. And sometimes outside of the school, if a crony of the Cromwells needed cheap labour.

Bea had found it a depressing experience, and had almost reached the point of giving up teaching altogether, when the chance came, unexpectedly, through a newspaper advertisement, to teach abroad.

With no hesitation she accepted the offer; and took a temporary job at another school while waiting for travel arrangements to be made. Since then, she had tasted freedom. Freedom to teach in her own way had been exhilarating. Now Mary-Ann had gone, and the kids needed her more than ever.

The mule quickened its pace, jerking her forward. Gardiner made no effort to control the animal; it amused him to make Beatrice run.

'I imagine the beast can smell home, Beatrice. I can see the end of the track, so we'll soon be there.'

She got her breath back where the ground levelled, and leaned back on the rope to slow the mule. Prairie grass extended before her, and she could see a group of wooden huts.

★ ★ ★

Savage had guessed what was coming and fell forward, twisting his body sideways as Parker fired his revolver. The slug caught him high in the shoulder and knocked him flat. He lay face down on the deck, motionless, as Parker swept past, screaming, 'Kill the vigilantes — don't spare any of them!'

Outlaws swarmed over the *New Victoria*. On the crowded deck it was close fighting with revolvers and knives. Miners and crewmen struggled hand-to-hand to save their lives.

A wild rage filled the raiders over Spike's hanging; the miners knew a desperate fear. And Savage kept his head down as the battle raged around him. The canted deck was slippery with blood and cartridge cases as the boat swung slowly in the current.

Amid the slaughter, Savage cautiously checked the shotgun Parker had pushed into his hands; it was empty, but he still had the knife in his belt. His shoulder throbbed, but he was alive.

The outlaws had an advantage. He saw Nate cutting and slashing with a huge Bowie knife, and sniffed the stink of gunfire; men cried out as they went down, while Parker raged: 'Kill! Kill them all!'

It was butchery. A small miner was trying to reload his gun and shouting, 'Jeff, help me,' before he was cut almost in half by the blast from a shotgun.

There was confusion as men fought for their lives amid the crackle of flames; dense smoke choked and blinded them.

A furious hail of bullets swept the deck. The boat sank deeper, and men jumped overboard. One shouted, 'I can't swim,' and submerged, spluttering.

The massacre was almost over. One of the rivermen was still upright and fighting until two of the raiders forced him backwards across a deck rail while a third gutted him the way he would a fish.

Savage moved warily, crawling between bodies; he was ignored by the looters, who were ransacking the dead and finishing off the wounded. Grasping hands searched feverishly for bags and pouches of dust and nuggets of gold.

He felt a need to return violence with violence, a greed for revenge, but at this moment, he could not see Foxy Parker through the swirling smoke. Then he realized it wasn't all smoke; some of the cloud obscuring the view was steam, hissing and scalding. The *New Victoria* still had pressure in her boiler.

Teeth bared in a fierce grin, he edged towards the boiler. He saw a coil of rope beside a hatchway, and cut a length, shoved the knife back in his belt and crawled on. He reached the smokestacks and staggered upright; a steam pipe came up from the boiler below, a safety valve on its top. Steam hissed and sprayed, and the metal was hot enough to take skin off. Careful not to touch it, he looped a length of rope over the valve lever and pulled down hard.

He almost tripped on a body, then slipped the rope under the corpse and tied it fast; he had the dead weight he needed.

Now that the valve was closed, the steam was unable to escape and pressure was building. Savage grinned ferociously as he thought: let's see how Parker's lot like that.

He stumbled towards the rail and fell over it towards the blood-reddened water.

A howl of 'Savage!' from behind

revealed that Foxy Parker had seen him; and the outlaw leader jumped after him.

As he hit the river, Savage heard an ear-splitting roar. The metal boiler exploded, sending death-dealing shards of metal and scalding steam across the open deck. He went deep, cutting off the screams.

★ ★ ★

'Stop that, Tom!'

Young Luke was beginning to wish Miss Beatrice hadn't left him in charge of the class. He wanted her to read to him, and liked the idea of learning to read for himself, but being a favourite put him on the spot.

Tom was one of the bigger boys, a bit of a bully, and just now was throwing pine cones at the prettiest girl in the schoolroom.

'Make me!' Tom challenged, and sneered, 'Teacher's pet.'

Luke was wondering what to do

when he heard a shot outside. With a feeling of relief, he left his place and crossed to the window.

He was startled to see the Englishman out of the cage, and Mary-Ann stretched out on the ground with Miss Beatrice kneeling beside her. His teacher's face was pale and showed strain as she came to her feet and accused Gardiner: 'You — murderer!'

Gardiner showed little reaction till after he'd reloaded his gun; then he hit her.

Voices behind him called, 'What's going on, Luke?' and there was a rush to the window.

Gardiner looped a rope around Bea's wrists and set his mule moving down the hill trail, dragging her after him.

Luke recovered from the shock. 'Tom,' he said, 'get your Ma to see after Mary-Ann — that English bastard shot her!'

He ran to the corral, straddled a horse and headed down the track to the river. Foxy needed to know about this.

He let the horse run, clinging to its mane, his legs clamped tight to its sides and his head down. He didn't have to guide his mount; all their horses knew the hill trails.

It was a shame about Mary-Ann, but it was the thought of losing his teacher that really worried him. He urged his horse to go faster.

The animal slithered on a patch of mud, recovered, and charged on down. Where the trees thinned out, Luke saw a red glow and smelt smoke.

He was almost to the river when a violent explosion bent tree trunks, shook branches and shredded leaves.

16

The Kill

When Savage surfaced, the air seemed strangely silent. He soon found he was out of his depth, and concentrated on dog-paddling to keep his nose and mouth above water.

As his hearing returned, he heard the rush of water swirling past, and a weak voice calling for help. A pall of smoke drifted across the river, shrouding the trees with grey. The wreck of the *New Victoria* lay canted at an angle, and dead bodies were being carried away on the current. One he recognized: it was Oscar.

At first glance it looked as though few of the gang had survived the explosion; which, he decided, was justice of a kind because few of the miners or crew had survived the massacre.

Even though a hot sun was beating down, he felt chilled and numb; then he remembered the river water was in flood from the snow-melt.

He turned through a circle, looking everywhere; he spotted Nate's body, tangled in some rigging, bobbing up and down. Parker had jumped after him, so where was he?

Then he saw him, clinging to a lump of timber blasted from the wreck. He was alive, and the way he hung on suggested he was a poor swimmer. Savage bared his teeth and went after him.

He remembered Parker putting him in a cage and leaving him to roast in the sun, without water; now Parker was up to his neck in freezing water.

Getting to him was not easy. His left shoulder hurt with each movement, and the current was strong, but he persisted in the hunt.

At bay, Parker watched him, holding on with one hand and aiming a revolver. He squeezed the trigger, and the cartridge misfired.

He tried another chamber, but Savage, knife in hand, reached him before he could fire. He slashed at the hand clutching the floating timber. Parker dropped his gun and lunged to get a grip with his other hand.

'Don't be a fool, Savage,' he gasped. 'I'll deal you in — '

Savage didn't bother to answer. It was *revenge* he wanted.

'I've a cache of gold hidden away. I'll share it with you.'

Savage slashed at his other hand, the one gripping the lump of timber. With Parker gone, he could help himself to as much gold as he could carry.

He thrust his knife back in his belt, grabbed Parker's legs and pulled him clear of the timber. They submerged and bobbed up, locked together in a death struggle.

Desperately Parker tried to climb on top, hitting Savage weakly with one hand, holding on with the other. It wasn't hanging he was afraid of now.

Savage's shoulder was bleeding freely. He took a long breath and ducked beneath the surface, taking Parker under with him. The Fox didn't have enough air in his lungs and opened his mouth, taking in water.

Savage stayed under till the fight went out of Foxy. When he surfaced, he kept Parker face down in the river till he was sure life was extinct.

★   ★   ★

Dave Bridger sat brooding; Savage should have been back by now. He was sleepy, and had shifted from whiskey to coffee, black and sweet. Maybe something had happened to the kid; maybe he wouldn't be back? What would he do then?

The card-players had left when the storm ended. Chandler was behind his counter, saying nothing, apparently absorbed in paperwork. His helper, dressed as a cowboy, was back; Bridger daren't ask him if he'd seen Savage, who was supposed to be asleep in the hut.

The cowboy, equally silent, sat on his own at another table with a deck of cards, laying them down one at a time with an air of deliberation, sometimes moving one on top of another.

Bridger found himself staring at a poster on the wall of the store; it advertised a pipe tobacco, and there was something hypnotic about the image. He wondered if he should try a pipe.

Then he heard sounds of an arrival and looked expectant towards the doorway. Was Savage coming at last?

But it was a woman who entered, stumbling as if she'd been pushed. She stood still a moment, rubbing her wrists and staring about the store as if she'd never seen the place before. Bridger noted the rope burns on her wrists and raised an eyebrow.

A man followed her in, a smirk on his face, and Bridge recognized him instantly. It was the man who'd called himself Winston and taken the supervisor's place at Fremont, and he was wanted for murder by the agency.

He came upright from his chair, drawing his gun in one easy movement. 'I want you — '

The killer ducked behind the woman, using her as a shield. He barked a laugh and called to Chandler, 'This here's a Pinkerton.'

Chandler appeared to hesitate, then nodded. Bridger felt a ring of cold metal pressed hard just behind his ear.

'Drop it, friend, or I'll drop you.'

The cowboy had moved quietly and was close behind, holding a revolver against Bridger's head.

Bridger wanted Winston's killer badly, but couldn't take the risk of hitting the woman. Cursing, he let his gun drop from his hand.

Chandler said, 'That's better. Remember, I'm the law here, even if you are a Pinkerton. Mr Gardiner, you relax too.'

'I can do that if you'll pass me a

decent cigar — I haven't had a smoke for hours.'

After Gardiner had got his cigar going, Chandler said solemnly, 'Now, let's have a bit of decorum. Mr Gardiner has paid in advance for a ceremony of marriage. Is this the lady?'

Gardiner blew a smoke ring, and nodded.

'And I shall be officiating almost immediately. I want no interruptions.'

Gardiner tightened his hold on Bea, who appealed directly to Bridger. 'Can't you do something to stop this farce? Mr Savage said you'd help me.'

'Where is he?'

'A prisoner of Mr Parker, unfortunately. I'm afraid his life is threatened.'

'Keep quiet, woman,' Chandler snapped. 'Such matters are not your concern. I'm sure Mr Parker can manage. Mr Gardiner, are you ready to proceed?'

'I'm ready — so is she.'

'Very good.' Chandler addressed Dave Bridger. 'Will you stand as witness?'

Before he could answer, Bea, struggling to free herself, shouted, 'No, he won't! I'm not going to marry this man. He's a murderer — he shot Mary-Ann!'

* * *

Savage felt exhausted and barely made it to the river-bank. He grasped an overhanging branch and paused to catch his breath. With a final effort, he hauled himself out of the water and collapsed on the bank.

After a few minutes, the sun warmed him and he gave his attention to the wreck of the *New Victoria*. There were no signs of life; surely they couldn't all have been killed? He had to assume any survivors had been washed away downstream.

He watched the river flow swiftly past; the current was strong. He was beginning to revive in the sun, becoming aware of his shoulder hurting, when hoofbeats pounded on the trail leading down from the hilltop.

He couldn't be bothered to move himself; just gripped the haft of his knife and waited.

The rider was a boy, freckle-faced, and Savage had a memory of seeing him around the school-teacher. The boy looked at the wreck and the empty river, puzzled. He approached Savage and asked, 'Where's Foxy?'

'Gone,' Savage murmured. 'They're all gone. The ship's boiler blew, and, as far as I can tell, I'm the only one left.'

The boy stared at him in silence, hardly believing. 'My name's Luke,' he said, 'and it's about Miss Beatrice. She's been taken to Chandler's — and you've got to save her.'

'Not me,' Savage said. 'I'm about done in.'

Luke regarded him with scorn. 'Some hero you are!'

'There aren't any heroes,' Savage told him. 'That's storybook stuff.'

Luke began badgering him. 'There's only you, so you've *got* to help. She saved you when you were in the cage, and now that Gardiner's got her — '

Savage sat up. 'Gardiner? He's out of the cage?'

'Yes, the Englishman. Miss Beatrice let him out, the way she did you. Then he shot Mary-Ann and dragged Miss Beatrice at the end of a rope down to Chandler's store. You've got to rescue her!'

Savage felt new life surge through him. Gardiner, the fake Winston who'd made a fool of him, getting away. He wanted to get his hands on that one; as he started to move, pain shot through his shoulder.

'D'you know how to bind up a shoulder, Luke?'

''Course I do! Think I've never seen a bullet-hole before?'

Luke washed the blood away with river water. 'Bullet's torn out a lump of flesh, that's all.' He made a pad to cover the hole, and bound it with a strip of shirt. 'Miss Bea — '

'She needn't worry, once I catch up with Gardiner.'

Luke brought one of the gang's horses and Savage climbed into the saddle.

'Follow me,' the boy shouted, and set off along the river-bank at a gallop.

17

Ladykiller

'Mary-Ann?' Chandler glanced at Gardiner. 'Mr Parker won't like that.'

Gardiner's smile held the chill of ice. 'It was necessary, old boy. Self-defence, you know? My bride forgot to mention that the woman was coming at me with a meat cleaver. But I intend to be gone before Mr Parker finds out, so can we get on?'

A cool one, with his fair hair and neat moustache, Chandler thought. 'Maybe we'd better.'

Dave Bridger, watching Gardiner's face, saw only a casual cruelty in the pale blue eyes, and suddenly knew that this woman's life hung by a thread. Once before, in New York, he'd met a man like this: a woman-killer, who married for money and murdered his wife, then married and murdered again, and —

'Mr Chandler,' he said urgently, 'if you marry them, you are condemning the woman to an early death. It's her money he's after — she may not know it — but once he's in a position to inherit, he'll — '

Chandler glared at him, then nodded a second time. The pressure eased from behind Bridger's ear as the cowboy lifted the barrel of his revolver and brought it down hard. Bridger reeled.

He stood, swaying, then the pressure was back.

'Best to keep quiet, friend,' the cowboy advised.

Chandler hummed a few bars of 'Here Comes the Bride'.

'Thank you, Shepherd. Now perhaps we can proceed without further interruption? Mr Gardiner, do you take this woman as your lawful wife?'

'I do.'

Bea kicked backwards and shouted, 'You can't force me to — '

Gardiner bent one of her fingers back till the bone snapped and she cried out in pain. 'I can break each one in turn,' he said quietly. 'It's up to you.'

'You're mad,' she said, 'if you think I'll — '

'Be silent, woman,' Chandler thundered. 'The Good Book commands a woman to be obedient. It says that a wife submits in all things to her husband. It lays down the law that your husband shall rule over you.'

Bea held her broken finger and hacked at Gardiner's shinbone. She was feeling contrary.

'When I was a sea captain,' Chandler boomed, 'I believed we were all equal in His eyes. Now I have come to believe that some are more equal than others. For instance, woman is created for man. His word is your authority. He leads and you follow . . . Mr Gardiner, do you have the ring?'

Gardiner sighed. 'Unfortunately, Mr Parker took it.'

Chandler beamed. 'Then it's lucky I

have a spare! That'll be five dollars.'

Gardiner paid, still holding a furious Bea, and the storekeeper produced a gold ring.

'Do you take this man for your lawful husband, in holy matrimony, to love, honour and obey?'

'Never!'

Gardiner blew on the end of his cigar till it glowed red, and then held it to her face. 'I advise you to change your answer,' he said softly, 'or I'll blind you in one eye.'

From outside came the sound of horses arriving.

★　★　★

Savage was losing blood and his shoulder was sore. Only the movement of the horse as he tried to keep up with Luke kept him awake; that and a gnawing need to settle his account with Gardiner. Nobody made a fool of him and got away with it. Afterwards, he thought, he might sleep for a week.

Luke pounded along the rough track beside the river, leaving the cotton-woods behind and heading out across the prairie. The teacher seemed to have made an impression on this boy, Savage thought, gripping his saddle horn.

By the time he saw the buildings making up Chandler's crosstrails store, he had little energy left. But if Gardiner got away now, he might never find him. Then he remembered he'd left Dave Bridger at the store.

Let Bridger delay the Englishman long enough for him to get there. A canteen hung by the saddle of his borrowed mount, and he drank to revive himself. When they came to a halt beside the main building, he slid from the saddle and clung to the horse to stay upright.

Chandler's voice droned from the doorway, and then Gardiner's. Savage grinned as he realized he was in time. He murmured to Luke, 'Show yourself at the front — I'll try the back way.'

He took a breath to prepare himself

and touched the knife at his belt. He walked unsteadily around the side of the store to another door, which was closed but not locked. He opened it and stepped inside.

A dusty light showed a stack of empty crates and old boxes, and he eased a way between, trying not to disturb them. He moved along a passage to another door and opened it gently. Where was Bridger?

Luke's voice reached him. 'You can stop worrying, Miss Beatrice. I've brought — '

Chandler snapped, 'Quiet, boy! This is a solemn occasion and I will not tolerate any interference.'

Savage heard the teacher shouting and saw her struggling to break free of the Englishman, who was holding a lighted cigar. Bridger had been disarmed, and the cowboy was standing behind him, a gun in his hand.

As he stepped into the open, Savage accidentally knocked against a water cistern, and it rang like a bell, attracting the attention of everyone in the store.

Dave Bridger took advantage of the distraction to whirl about and hit the cowboy, then dive to the floor after his gun.

Chandler stepped back hastily, wary of being caught in a crossfire. A gold ring hit the boards and rolled away.

Gardiner stared blankly until comprehension came. Then he recognized Savage, whose face was white and strained and streaked with blood, and was apparently without a weapon. He laughed. 'The jailbird! Got away from Foxy, did you?'

He pushed Bea from him to get a clear shot, pulled his derringer from inside his coat and aimed.

Bea staggered, off-balance, and struggled to get back at Gardiner, but knew she would be too late to save Savage.

A stage magician could not have timed it better. Mysteriously, a knife appeared in the hand of Savage. Gardiner squeezed the trigger as the knife became a blur of steel hurtling through the air.

Savage stumbled as the slug tore open his bandaged shoulder.

Gardiner was knocked backwards, the gun falling from his hand. He stared at the ceiling, the haft of a knife projecting from his throat.

He made a gurgling sound, 'Savage . . . you . . . ' and slumped back with only a bloody froth bubbling from his lips.

A silence lasted until Beatrice picked up the gold ring and looked thoughtfully at Savage. She saw him slump into a chair, his eyes closing, and nudged the cowboy. 'Hot water and a bandage, quickly.'

'Yes, ma'am.'

Dave Bridger snorted. 'He'll survive!'

Luke said, wistfully, 'Will you be coming back to our school, Miss?'

Chandler moved behind his counter, lowered the flap and beamed at them all.

'Waal, now that's settled, maybe you

folks fancy a drink? I've got the usual, or I can manage champagne if you feel like celebrating. For those with an appetite, I can provide ham and eggs.'

He nodded towards Gardiner, who was stretched out on the floor.

'So while I rustle up drinks, or a meal, you can decide between you who's going to pay for the burial.'

THE END

We do hope that you have enjoyed reading this large print book.

Did you know that all of our titles are available for purchase?

We publish a wide range of high quality large print books including:
Romances, Mysteries, Classics
General Fiction
Non Fiction and Westerns

Special interest titles available in large print are:
The Little Oxford Dictionary
Music Book, Song Book
Hymn Book, Service Book

Also available from us courtesy of Oxford University Press:
Young Readers' Dictionary
(large print edition)
Young Readers' Thesaurus
(large print edition)

For further information or a free brochure, please contact us at:
Ulverscroft Large Print Books Ltd.,
The Green, Bradgate Road, Anstey,
Leicester, LE7 7FU, England.
Tel: (00 44) **0116 236 4325**
Fax: (00 44) **0116 234 0205**